Fearkiller

by

Chris Maley

Library of Congress Cataloging-in-Publication Data

Maley, Chris
Fearkiller

ISBN-10: 0615574572
EAN-13: 978-0615574578

www.amazingcookiepress.com
www.chrismaley.com

Cover Art by Justin Hayes

Photo: David Pahl, David Pahl Photography

Library of Congress Control Number: 2012935816
Fearkiller, Denver, CO

Fearkiller

by

Chris Maley

To a small group of friends who read earlier, convoluted drafts of this and gave me their thoughts: thanks for the good, the bad, and every what-were-you-thinking-here-because-frankly-I-have-no-idea-whatsoever. Since this was my first time doing this, I can't tell you how much your feedback was appreciated.

For Lisa, Kathy, Justin, Jim, Lindsey, Ann, and my brother Merlin.

Justin, thanks for the cover, rocking that idea to life.

And David my friend, thank you for my photo.

There is no illusion greater than fear
—Lao Tzu, *Tao Te Ching,* 4th Century, B.C.

EGAN

I

Note to Old You.

Some type of song exists somewhere.

It's about knowing what we know now. Today. Only back then, yesterday. When we weren't as old as we are now. When we were younger.

It's a song about regret.

Can't remember the exact words, but the idea in this song is about regret. Maybe this song is about destroying regret the nanosecond before it destroyed you.

From the back room, Egan yells that he's sorry I feel this way.

Songs about destroying regret. There should be more songs about destroying regret. From this point forward, this feeling will no longer be a part of this story. Fear is the main character.

Live music. You and Old You share a bond through live music.

From the back room, Egan is communicating that he is sorry for the way I feel right now.

Where's the remote? Seen this episode a gazillion times. Egan is sorry.

Click. "And The Fear Index is holding steady—" the newscaster says, from behind his desk.

Thanks, Mr. Newscaster, breakthrough journalism at its finest.

"Hey, Egan, The Fear Index is holding steady," I yell. "I thought you could use some good news." Click.

Wait—I thought this game was on tomorrow night. Sweet.

"I'm sorry that you feel this way. But think of my kids."

Egan is again using his three children to justify why he shouldn't be beaten to death with a hammer. The same children who inspired him to have affairs with other women while his wife was pregnant with them or raising them. Egan is using those children to justify why he should live.

Hey SuperDad: your youngest one, the day you told everyone that your wife was pregnant again, how did you announce this news?

"If it's another girl, I'll sell her to an A-rab or some Chink." Chuckle, chuckle.

Didn't you say that? Sure, it was a joke, but didn't you say that? Chuckle, chuckle.

"Please, think of my kids—"

"Shut up. We *are* thinking of your kids."

Know what's funny here? Egan the Exec inspired this whole crazy adventure, with his combination of ineptitude, leading by fear instead of leading by example, destroying departments then justifying things by recommending layoffs, then causing more destruction with each promotion from Corporate—all with that entitled smirk on his face.

But Egan the Family Man is, the more you think about it, contributing to this plan as well. Harassed women aside, us workers got the better end of the deal.

That guy is the vision of success in the year 2010. How did the world get to the point where he is a vision of success?

"I'm sorry that you feel this way."

He's pleading for help again—no—he's trying to guilt-trip me into stopping all of this. Telling me that I have to think—not of him, but—of his kids.

Egan, around the office you sure weren't afraid to bring up the expensiveness of your kids. Or how your wife's ass used to look before your kids. Then you would switch gears and kill productivity or—

"Egan: sorry to talk work for a sec, but remember ignoring that customer's directive, then shifting the blame to the Phoenix office? Two people lost their jobs, you know."

At its core, ego is fearful, panicky, ignorant, miserable, doubtful, and uncertain.

Yet manifested correctly, ego is embraced and righteously unleashed. Because our world embraces and worships fear, panic, ignorance, misery, doubt, and uncertainty—even ruthlessness, relentlessness and remorselessness—more and more each day.

Open up a newspaper. Scan the headlines for a bit. See?

Egan: physical discomfort aside, this must feel so honest compared to, say, setting up Sharon and Stevie to be fired.

"And admit it: part of the reason for the fearmongering was to smokescreen the fact that you had zero idea what you were doing. Ferocity masking inferiority."

Part of what makes this whole hammer-death-beating adventure so fun is that it puts into action those intimations and words Egan wielded to hurt others.

His fear, turned back at him. That intimidating yet empty threatening stance, we're breathing some air into that stance and redirecting all of it right back at Egan.

Him trying to appear composed. It highlights how seriously he takes the concept of himself. Of Egan. It's almost like Egan® or something.

And *drop* this whole 'ruining-those-kids'-lives' thing, dude. More than one perfectly fine adult grew up without both parents. And many kids who grew up with both parents became detriments to society.

"Dylan Klebold and Eric Harris each had two married parents. So did Jeffrey Dahmer. Ted Bundy and Charles Manson's fathers disappeared when they were young. And countless other kids in both of these situations grew up just fine. Sound complicated? This is life. That crazy little thing called life. Your logic, it's flawed."

Besides, 'A-rab or some Chink'? Seriously?

Egan was one of those white guys who would say something offensive in the guise of a joke—a black joke to a black guy, a blonde joke to a blonde. All very offensive, then he'd pull out the "I was just joking." Or, "HEY. It was a joke…" if this didn't appear to appease things.

"How did you not only manage to keep your job after the SuperCompa customer firing us for your oversights, but get a promotion as well?"

Though in all honesty I'll admit that even though he destroyed our grandkids' futures, Egan and people like him got shit done. I didn't.

So, one day, I decided—no—I had an epiphany.

I looked at myself in the mirror and said: I wanna do something. Be somebody.

I wanna strut down the street and have people wave and say, "Heyyyyy! It's the guy who beat Egan to death with a hammer! You da man, dude! The economy is rawking—I got two job offers today!"

And as I strutted I'd respond with a wink, a finger-gun-click, and a "Backatcha, babe!"

Here's what I want: I want to be at the apex of a phalanx of ecstatic working-class folks screaming my name.

All of us running down the street, me in a pair of grey sweats, wool hat, arms raised in the air at the head of the working-class-folk phalanx, everyone high-fiving and fist-pounding, jumping on and diving off the roof of cars, all the while the economy rocking, then rocking even more, then rocking even more.

Everyone, at some point in life, no matter their race, creed, gender, etc., should experience what it is like at the apex of a phalanx of ecstatic, working-class folks.

Me. The tip of the spear. Leading this people-phalanx down the street and our economy upward.

I wanna go the distance.

Egan knew how to go out in the world and be somebody. Now I'm stealing a page from that playbook—bullshit. I'm writing a *new* playbook—

Know what? Egan fucked over way more than the working-class people. Shit, anybody that's been fucked over by Egan or men like him in any way shape or form—

All of those people, screaming my name, cheering me on. Afterward, I wanna sign autographs.

True: I began this millennium face-down, passed out on the floor of a laundry room, keeping an eye out for Y2K and signs of the end of civilization. And since then, in those ten years, it all lead me here.

To the point where I'm about to beat one of the worlds' worst executives to death with a hammer.

A guy that, if he was the same chip-on-shoulder, entitled prick he is today, only he was good at managing and leading people and getting them to perform, wouldn't be here. That guy, though he would be an asshole, would be alive and well.

Egan? He only had the fearmongering part down. The revenue-generation and help-people-do-their-jobs-better things, not so much.

See, this hammer death beating isn't a personal attack. It's professional.

Compile a true performance review for Egan, not the one the world writes for him to make shareholders happy. Look at Egan's actual numbers. See? This is just a business decision.

It's the year 2010. Everything he screwed up, every time a harassment claim was filed, he ended up positively benefiting from the negativity he created.

And then an economy crashed. He still benefited.

A man that is living proof that the system is rigged and it benefits a few—even those who are poor performers—more than most. Well, I'm about to murder him.

Then I'm going to feed his body parts into a wood chipper I'll park by the shore of a secluded little cove on the lake.

It's off-season, so with the rainy weather and all, I'm not expecting company out there. Once I'm done, I'll push the wood chipper into the lake at this spot close to shore where the bottom drops off kind of suddenly. It's a little spot I discovered years ago, on a picnic with people who no longer speak to me.

The cove itself is secluded, and boaters avoid it with the sandbars. The drop-off itself should send the wood chipper say, ten feet down. I give it at least a few years of anonymity. And by then, if it ever does get discovered, Mother Nature will have taken care of any last traces of Egan.

Somebody has to try and save this economy. Maybe this will—

Wait. I don't know how much longer I'll be around after Egan is gone. Old You deserves an explanation though.

Before we go any further, think about two things:

One: Learning how to properly state "I don't know" is the path to success in this millennium.

Two: Embrace fear. Once you do, you will go far.

Yeah, a wood chipper. For the job it needs to do, it's efficient.

The world is obsessed with finding efficiencies nowadays.

2

"I'm sorry that you feel this way."

The state you're in now, Egan, at another point in time, this would have disgusted me. But now it makes me want to capture as much of each moment as possible.

I'm positive some frame of reference will reveal itself. It will either materialize for somebody else or it will guide me to—wait, I don't care what lies down this path.

But I have faith that this world will right itself soon. I'm certain this world will right itself soon.

Intriguing: so many people who aren't about to murder somebody have given up all hope for the future of our planet. They've abandoned optimism.

I couldn't believe in the human race more right now if I tried.

Quit believing in yourself. It opens your eyes to other possibilities—

"Please..."

For some reason, I blurt out "Thank you" as an answer to Egan's "Please."

Mainly to cut "Dad" off before he brings up his kids. And it's the funniest thing ever said.

A couple of minutes later—I think—I'm still on the ground rolling. If my ribs were made of more brittle tissue, I would have broken them by now, laughing that hard.

Part of what was so funny is the whole how-you-were-raised, that "manners" thing.

Say "please." Answer with "thank you".

"…plea…please"

"*Thank you.*"

Those comedians from my youth, the ones that taught me how to use the f word. The ones that weren't comedians, but poets, the way they used profanity.

Right now my laughing rivals those moments in time when I heard those tapes.

It's like I'm nine years old again, my buddy's older brother is away and we snuck into his room to play the tapes.

Those jokes, to a nine-year-old, the profanity itself was twice as funny as the joke—

FUCKSHITDAMNDICKHEADPUSSYMOTHERFUCKERFART SHIT—

Nine-year-olds, hearing this comedy for the first time, rolling on the floor.

That's me right now.

"Please—"

"THANKYOUFUCKSHITDAMNDICKHEADPUSSYMOTHER FUCKERFARTSHIT."

Keep the comedy coming. That kid, from years ago, what's he doing now? He moved away when we were twelve.

"I'm sorry you feel the way you do. But think of—"

Hey Egan, didn't you tell that stripper with a kid that her kid and your kids would make great step-siblings, even if she was a complete skank? You called her infant daughter "skank child" just to see if she would still grind on you after you laid down a fifty-dollar bill.

Skank child?

"Please, think of my—"

Fuckstain: I *am* thinking of your kids.

Pointing out the stripper's stretch marks, asking her if she was going to train her daughter to work the pole, or would she let some other filthy cunt teach her?

Then another fifty, and her grinding on you.

"Please—"

"THANK YOU FOR STINKING UP MY PLACE, FEAR-MONGER."

"…please…"

"THANK YOU FOR DOUBT, FEAR, PANIC, UNCERTAINTY, MISERY, IGNORANCE, AND YOUR MANAGEMENT TOOLS, YOU INCOMPETENT. THAT WHOLE DEPARTMENT GOT THE AXE BECAUSE OF YOU. YOUR FUCKED-UP BONUS—"

"p…plea…pleeth…"

"THANK YOU FOR BLINDSIDING PAM SCHOBERLE AND JENNIFER SMYTHE BECAUSE THEY WOULDN'T FUCK YOU. YOU GOT OFF ON IT. YOU STUPID INSECURE ALL TERRIFIED, THANK YOU FOR GETTING SCHOBIE AND JEN RAIL-ROADED OUT. AND STEVIE AND MILLER AND SHARON FIRED, THEY WERE NATURAL LEADERS—PEOPLE LISTENED TO THEM—MENTORS HAD OUR BACKS. YOU STOMPEDSTOMPED INITIATIVE. YOU FUCKED OVER TWO WHOLE DEPART—YOU ARE A CORPORATE WELFARE CASE. EVERY PAYCHECK YOU TAKE HOME IS LIKE A FUCKING HANDOUT BECAUSE YOU GOT PAID EVEN THOUGH EVERYTHING YOU OVERSAW TURNED TO SHIT YOU GOT PROMOTED AND TOO STUPID SHIT-FOR-BRAINS TO HAVE EARNED EVERY PENNY YOU EVER EARNED ALL A FUCKING HANDOUT DO YOU EVEN THINK OF ALL THOSE THAT GOT LAID OFF INSECURE ENTITLED LITTLE— GOOD PEOPLE GOT THE AXE YOU GOT PROMOTED ASSHOLES LIKE YOU TALK ALL SURVIVAL OF THE FITTEST BUT YOU'D LAST LIKE FIVE MINUTES IN THE WILD DROP THAT BULLSHIT ACT—"

Pain. My foot. Shit. Could've sworn I was wearing steel-toed flight boots.

I limp back to the front room. Couch time. If this were another point in time, I would tell myself that I need to work on my professionalism.

☆　☆　☆

Egan's pretty far gone.

I laid down to rest and could have been sleeping for twenty minutes or twenty days, I don't know.

How much presence of mind is still present in our friend Egan? Will he come to his senses and hate me?

I'd hate me. I'm being a dick right now. But he is still, when coherent, using his kids. His three burdens. And give him credit, he didn't sell the third to an A-rab or some Chink.

Get over yourself, Egan.

Dude, grow some balls. Revolt.

Those things you used to say about Connie, the receptionist, just because her husband was black. That hateful energy in your jokes, bring that viciousness now.

You thought you owned fear, only fear owned you. Just admit this. Then again, not admitting mistakes helped ruin our country. Why we are where we are in 2010.

Way to be patriotic, dude. That's why you advanced. And it's why you aren't much longer for this Earth.

I gotta run a quick errand, then it is best that we take care of this.

It will be kind of like a layoff. We make a clean break and move on.

As far as the wood chipper for disposal goes, it may be gruesome but you have to give me credit for my professionalism here. For the job it needs to do, it's quick and efficient. Again, this is a business decision.

Egan: you spent your whole life attempting to wield and manipulate that entity known as fear. You climbed the ladder on the back of that thing you called fear. Fear was your weapon. Fear smokescreened so many mistakes. Fear masked your ineptitude and the fact that your position of leadership was 100 percent unearned and you were a complete failure.

Fear, in the end, was man-handling you the entire time.

Yet you can't acknowledge this fact. Humble yourself a bit. You could be free now—with these kids who suddenly became so much more important now that you might be beaten to death—if you just leveled yourself.

A lot of what is being done here is taking your words, your language, your threats, and turning them into action.

This is called calling your bluff.

This could have ended much more positively.

You shit the bed.

3

Egan, thirty-ish-or-forty-maybe-fiftyish, of Denver, Colorado, died Saturday, February 23rd, 2010. He is survived by who knows. Obviously some kids because he wouldn't quit kvetching about those pint-sized burdens ruining his game with the strippers. His third daughter, yeah, he had this joke—you know, let's not revisit that foul idea he thought of as a joke. Yeah, that fearmonger EVP, who stifled initiative and screwed up whole departments then got promoted, was one of those douche-pricks who felt the need to reproduce, even though his offspring sucked away all his money. He is survived by all those who got laid off to cover his—here you go: he was like those platoon lieutenants in Vietnam who got fragged by their own soldiers for being incompetent. He'd be a frag magnet over there. Egan also left behind fear, doubt, uncertainty, ignorance, misery, and panic, with some dashes of ruthlessness, relentlessness, and remorselessness. He is survived by a decade that, in my opinion, might as well be called The I Don't Know Decade. Can you explain what happened? I didn't think so. Most likely Egan is survived by a parent or two. A brother and/or brothers and/or sister and/or sisters, probably, right? Maybe his grand-folks are still alive. But they're probably real old and gum little glass bowls of custard. We're digressing…he is also survived by a wife—whom he rarely mentioned as he was chained to the wall in his final days of life. Insensitive dick. Manners? Hello? Using your kids to try and guilt-trip me, and never once using your wife to try and guilt-trip me into not killing you? Serious dick move, dude. You demeaned her in life, yet couldn't even mention her in those final days of your life? At least buy her flowers or someth—oh yeah, you're dead. I'm such an amateurish obituary writer. Your wife was pregnant with your second kid while you had that affair with that bimbo Admin. The one they fired after finding out about you two. Supposedly this was all bad for company morale, but you didn't get fired. Hmmm. And you didn't even have the decency to mention this wife in those moments before I beat you to death with a hammer? Serious, dude—you are one serious dick. Chances are his wife will survive. I can't really remember her, but I'm betting she'll meet some other guy, and those kids will turn out all right. Maybe some new guy will come along that—me? What? Any chick that would, with that guy—are you serious? Really? Dude, bleccch. What else? Egan is survived by his SUV and that cockamamie dickhead bike he rode to work on Fridays. You. A biker. Really? If you could still look at yourself, you would need to take a long look at yourself. A biker? Really? Oh yeah, we can't forget those legions of harassed waitresses, strippers, retail saleswomen. And he's also survived by those other higher-ups. Hopefully at least some of this group saw through his disgusting, Great Recession-causing horseshit and just humored him or whatever. They gotta look out for the status quo. But if this entire group saw him but didn't see through him, what does this say about our world? Maybe that's the state of business, why America is spiraling downward. I'm answering my own question. Services will be held at Our Lady of The Lady Who Birthed Jesus, The Kicker Of Non-Believin' Heathen Ass. So it is, and so it shall be. Holy Moly chicken mole, or Holy canoli is my shoulder sore. Whatever those men in the black robes say. And then they wave their hand around in the air and light incense and everyone screams "Hiphiphooray!" or "Hallelujah!" at the top of their lungs then the whole group fist pounds or something. I should really call a doctor and see if they can look at my sore shoulder on such short notice.

4

"Doc, thanks for seeing me and looking at my sore shoulder on such short notice."

"Well, since I've been disbarred I have a lot of time on my hands—"

"Disbarred? You're a doctor, not a lawyer—"

"Yes. I know. Son, I am such an awful doctor that all the lawyers banded together and preemptively had me disbarred in order to stop me from even thinking of switching to law."

"And you have no problem with the fact that I beat Egan to death with a hammer, then got rid of his body using a wood chipper?"

"These are tough times we're in. Besides, I heard that Egan guy was a productivity-killing, micro-managing, incompetent prick. Now let's look at that shoulder. Hmmm. Before this hammer death beating, did you stretch?"

"Oh yes, Doc. I put in my yoga DVD and did the entire 'Stretch' section. Even jumped rope."

"That's odd. And as you were doing this, you're positive that an out-of-work builder or dot-bomber or Karl Rove didn't swoop in from the sky on an oversized black crow and beat you with a blunt object?"

"Very positive."

"And you're sure this Egan person is dead, after you threw his body parts into that wood chipper and all? It would be nice to ask him questions—"

"I beat Egan to death with a tack hamm—"

"Did you say a 'tack' hammer?"

"Well, yeah…"

"There you go! It's your rotator cuff, or possibly a pectoralis major tendon inflammation, because you're clueless about hammer weight and size. A *tack* hammer? You know what we medical professionals HATE? When people engage in some type of physical exertion without consulting a medical professional first! How many swings?"

"Gosh, Doc. I don't kn—"

"'I don't know' is not acceptable. Was it around thirty?"

"More, I think."

"Good *God,* man! How hard were you swinging?"

"Pretty hard, I guess."

"BuulllllSHIT, fucko. You *know* how hard you were swinging. Level with me."

"I gave it maybe ninety-eight percent—"

"Son, that was a brainfart of a hammer choice."

"It was on sale. I even picked it up in the store and yelled, 'HEY, IT WOULD BE AWESOME TO KILL EGAN WITH THIS.' I got a few thumbs-ups. Maybe the other customers were just thinking about gas prices or their dwindling retirement."

"Here's my advice: next time, buy a thirteen-ounce Light Duty hammer. Swings well. Gauging your size and body type, it should take you fifteen solid swings, maybe twenty. All landed in the right places, of course."

"A thirteen-ounce Light Duty. Hmmm—"

"Yup. But to tell you the truth, more I look at your shoulder, the more—raise your elbow, like this. Wait a minute. You've been shoveling bullshit, piles of bullshit, spinning your wheels, digging holes then filling them, reinventing the wheel—you're a member of the American workforce in the year 2010, aren't you, son?"

"Well, Doc, I've been through a bunch of layoffs and restructurings and the world is going crazy, if that's what you mean—"

"Yup, I knew it. You've been mainlining fear, doubt, panic, uncertainty, misery, and ignorance. The bullshittendonitis gave it away. No wonder you murdered that talentless/pointless executive. Your uncertainty—well, you're an Unpaid Overtimer, someone who just hurtled through that ignorance-riddled I Don't Know Decade. The Fear Index, The Misery

Index, both through the roof. Your levels of apprehensiveness regarding job security, last decade it got to the point where it became Job Suck-Curity, the IDK Decade brand of job security. I bet you regularly receive e-mails full of those silly little doubt-inducing ellipses points, '…'—"

"Every day, Doc, in pretty much every e-mail now. It's to the point where people can't even have electronic conversations anymore without those causing people to second-guess everything. Like…this…"

"*The Portland Manual of Style* states, 'ellipsis points, or ellipses, indicate hesitation or a broken sentence, often associated with and meant to hint at doubt, insecurity, unsure feelings, and uncertainty.'"

"Doubt…Insecurity…Unsure Feelings…Uncertainty…I worked for legions of people who turned these into managerial tools. Egan and all those underlings that followed him were pros at using those. They even now come across in people's voices—"

"Yes, son! For instance, when a supervisor says, 'We should have a chat,' I bet it now comes across infused with subtle undertones, you hear those ellipses when they speak. It's 'we…should…have a chat…' or 'you don't seem to be happy to work here…' 'Is there a problem?' becomes 'Is…there…a problem…?' They actually teach that delivery in business schools nowadays. Those ellipses…I think of them as verbal sniper bullets for chickenshits. *Dot!-dot!-dot!s*. See, back in my day, the regular mail day, one would never end correspondence with those doubt-inducing dotdotdots, '…' You talked through the point you wanted to make—But enough about me, here, this is about you. Son, I bet you're so panic-filled day in, day out that you're quite adept at dancing The Shit-Fucking Dance."

"The Shit-Fucking Dance?"

"Watch: Look at me! I fuck shit! Look at me! I fuck shit!"

"Good God, Doc, you just transformed into every person in my company during those months before the twenty-five percent layoff!"

"And watch this: Look! At! Me! I! Fuck! Shit! IFuckShitIFuckShit! Lookatme Lookatme Lookatme! Ifuckshit Ifuckshit Ifuckshit!"

"Doc: you *BECAME* the stressed-out, overworked, kept-in-the-dark-and-scared-for-their-jobs, Y2K-infected barbarian sex cannibal American workforce—just now!"

"And: LookatmeIfuckshitIfuckshitIfuckshitlookatmelookatmelookat me—"

"Doc, watching you spin around like that I just had a flashback of watching every manager and assistant manager I worked for in the previous decade standing in front of me and trying to explain what needed to be accomplished—"

"Son, around roughly June of 2009, the workforce broke down to the point where you all just began to repeat 'look at me I fuck shit' and dance that productivity-killing, continually-changing—"

"You mean we've been pants-shittily running around in circles like chickens with our heads off?"

"Son, don't insult those who pants-shittily run around in circles like chickens with their heads cut off. They have their shit together compared to the current American workforce. Those Unpaid Overtimers, dancing that logic-defying, profit-margin-destroying dance. One minute the dance steps are one-TWO-three-four, the next they're ONE-three-four-two, then that new VP starts and they're SEVEN-thirteen-NINE-four. You've been dancing The Shit-Fucking Dance instead of actually digging yourselves out of the economic crisis."

"Doc! The other day, a coworker said to me, 'Look at me! I fuck shit!' I dismissed it, I just assumed she wanted me to look at her because she was fucking shit or something, I didn't know it was this!"

"Son, that dance is the degeneration of workflow, those inefficient, ever-changing array of dance steps you all constantly dance due to lack of foresight, short-term vs. long-term thinking, mindlessly embracing the status quo. Each company technology upgrade, those microwave cell phones popping popcorn and emailing faxes of half-baked ideas, these socially-mediated upgrades sending each foot dancing off in opposite directions—some of you go crazy, even growing new feet to keep up and incorporate everything into the workflow process. The Shit-Fucking Dance exploded on the workplace scene when people's level of sensory overload and stress got so out of hand that they danced and stumbled around the office like panicky little zombie-toddlers, all hopped up on fear."

"Yes! Doc, I get it. When you just did those confusing dance steps it was like I had a PTSD-style flashback—"

"Son, don't disgrace our men and women in uniform by comparing their noble plight to The Shit-Fucking Dance. Show some respect. The out-of-control fearmongering during the I Don't Know Decade, our service people are better than that. The Shit-Fucking Dance happened because leadership wasn't doing its job."

"You're right, Doc, that was wrong of me. But when you started dancing those steps, gosh, it was like I was transported back to work—"

"Son, during the last decade the rise in the levels of ignorance, fear and uncertainty, the doubt, the panic and misery, the ruthlessness, relentlessness and remorselessness, they've changed all of us."

"I'm with you there. Do you think the world's preoccupation with fear could have started during those final years of the previous decade, stemming from our preoccupation with Y2K? Like our fixation on the end of civilization and the dates in our computers? Our focus on fear ten years later, maybe these are intertwined?"

"That's an interesting hypothesis, son. You know, a patient of mine was in fact victim number one of the Third Millennium, the very first person to die after we all crossed over. Y2K-related, an older fella, in his seventies. He was with his wife over at some friends' house, older couples who never stay up late. Anyway, five, four, three, two, one, HAPPY NEW MILLENNIUM. Then the light starts to flicker. Turns out the host was going to get that light switch looked at the week before, but forgot. My patient assumed the worst, of course, and was dead from a heart attack/brain aneurism just seven seconds into the Millennium."

"Sorry for snickering, Doc, that all just seems so funny now."

"Funny now? Try ten years ago. I accidentally burst out laughing when I sat down with his wife and heard the full story, just after it happened. It's a good thing you can now trade options on The Volatility Index, or Fear Index, or else I'd never make money these days. Did you know that starting February 24, 2006, you could buy Fear futures—a 'call' order if you're thinking more fear, and 'put' order if you're predicting less fear? VIX Options Contracts—"

"Making money on fear and people's outlook related to fear. Really?"

"Sure can, son. There's a Fear Index *and* a Misery Index. Capitalize on all that negativity out there. Implied volatility, git some. We don't make products. We make math formulas and call them products."

"Interesting perspective, Doc."

"For trading, I even got me a special double-sided policeman-style shoulder holster. Where the pistols normally go, I fill up the right side with a bunch of Fear Indexes, the left side up with a bunch of Misery Indexes—they're squirmy little fellers—then I throw on my black leather trenchcoat, oversized orange foam cowboy hat, and GIMME HEAD 'TIL I'M DEAD medallion. And I get to trading. That sinister guy over there's looking for a Misery Index, I reach inside the coat, double-pump, grab a Misery Index and fling it, WHAMMO—"

"What's interesting about all of this, Doc, is that I'm feeling that I should have reached out to a medical professional like yourself much earlier. Egan might be alive today."

"That's psychiatry, son. I'd offer my thoughts but I'm banned from practicing psychiatry, along with law and culinary arts. Your shoulder looks good, though. Now if you'll excuse me I'm going to go change into a baby diaper and bib and astronaut helmet and snort Mount Fujis of coke off my nurse's breasts. That nurse of mine loves Internet candid animal videos. Do you? Have you seen the one where the penguins invent the waste-free fusion reactor? Silly penguins. My receptionist has your paperwork up front, make sure everything is correct. Insurance companies are all pants-shitty about Obamacare."

5

Egan is in the lake. Fish food.

Been a while now.

Looked The Fear Index up. Doc was right.

The Fear Index trades on the idea of implied volatility. And when stocks go higher, the VIX goes lower.

Volatility. Implied.

Something else, every site I looked at said the same thing: the VIX has no *intrinsic* value. By itself, it's not worth anything at all.

Think about its commoditization during The I Don't Know Decade: creating trading options based on fear during a ten-year span that saw this same concept—fear—mutate and become more pervasive.

Add to this: IDK, that decade. Its foundation was laid by Y2K. Not only did the year 2000 begin the decade, but that potentially-civilization-ending technology glitch called Y2K laid the foundation for ten years where fear, doubt, ignorance, uncertainty, panic, and misery moved into our lives and said "We're taking over."

Implied volatility. With no intrinsic value. The Fear Index.

I may be on to something here.

Egan was an all-consuming project for so long, then I was going to end it all. Now I can't, so now thoughts of being caught, a new set of problems—and this new train of thought, The I Don't Know Decade, The Fear Index, Y2K, my overdue doctor's visit.

This whole adventure was meant to quiet everything, not amplify.

Instead, you are here, certain that The Fear Index is probably rising, implying volatility.

"Hey World! This is The Fear Index, implying that things *might* be volatile."

You are here, looking through a giant stack of mail that you would rather light on fire. Or just leave in a pile on the front porch so it doesn't take up space inside, but the neighbors might wonder.

These pieces of mail say things like Uncle Dave's surgery went okay, there's a sale on garden shears, one in six people are mentally ill, a sixteen-inch two-topping is just $10.99—

Back the truck up.

"One in six are mentally ill"? The fuck you get off sending literature to this address stating the Universe contains this phenomena called "mental illness"?

Hey, you Mental Illness Is Bad And Pants-Shitty people: about twelve years ago, you could have mailed me something.

Take this address off your mailing list.

Take a deep breath, you are here.

Still not quite knowing what to do with those sensations and visions of washing another person's blood off your body.

Near the end, his left eye gone. The right still there, eyelid no longer able to blink.

Human bones crack louder than chicken bones.

Blood.

Full-on terror, entitled smirk leaving his face forever.

Hammer connecting with Egan's temple. The rigid, then the soft part.

Egan in pain. He looked so out of his element.

Doc's insight, this tack hammer being too light.

When he started to scream, such a different sound.

Wasn't anticipating that, or the pain. Swinging that way-too-light hammer with everything you had, kicking, stomping though you were in running shoes not steel-toed flight boots.

Running behind schedule. Then getting back on schedule.

Out by the lake. The wood chipper. The Axeman showed up, suicide left.

Then.

And you are here. Now.

Which isn't then. Back then.

When you weren't as old as you are now.

No, not Egan's death. Let's go much farther back.

That bar, December 31st, 1999. 11:59:02.

Back then, waiting for that coke dealer. (Sketchy yet necessary bunch, coke dealers.) Fifty-eight seconds from Y2K.

Waiting for the clock to strike, for the explosions to begin.

Fifty-eight seconds from now, forget HAPPY NEW YEAR. We're talking HAPPY NEW MILLENNIUM—only every electric light might die, you're thinking. Then you're thinking that the coke dealer is late.

In the final minute of the entire millennium, when we all should be elated, starry-eyed to be alive on Podunk Planet Earth at this moment, Y2K and Fear's cone-shaped New Year's Eve party hat are the tempering forces.

Hey everybody! Let's say goodbye to a thousand years and welcome in a thousand brand new ones, apprehensively!

Because our computers didn't understand the concept of millennia and centuries, due to the omission of these two digits, there was a chance we might not cross over.

Y2K. Potentially shutting down electrical plants—no, the very concept of electricity itself. Goodbye hopes, dreams, worth. And once we devour all the prepared food and sodas in the walk-in refrigerators and storage pantries, those secret recipes that corporations guard with their lives will be gone forever.

The omission of two digits in a year of a line of computer code might trigger an outbreak of Y2K Innards-Falling-Out Syndrome, for all we knew.

Another scenario: the ball dropping in Times Square could release Y2K radiation. This was a government/corporation thing. Maybe this secretly-implanted radiation would infect us, turning all of us into those hordes of Y2K-infected barbarian sex cannibals.

Or maybe the Y2K fire-breathing flying brontosauruses would swoop in, incinerating every human being on Earth by January 4, 2000.

Who knew what was in store for us on the other side?

Who knows? This sparkling new canvas called The New Millennium is blank right now, at this moment in 1999.

And here's something to make you take a step back: all the potential disasters we were thinking about back then, we weren't thinking about planes flying into buildings.

And I don't know about you, but I couldn't fathom that concept back then. We were here.

About 85 percent starry-eyed to be alive at this moment in time. And 15 percent apprehensive.

Was it the Y2K bug, the computer glitch that was terrifying? Or was it the sheer unknown, The Third Millennium, diluted down into this anomaly, The Millennium Bug? Maybe Y2K threw us off course.

To put this another way: how much more starry-eyed would we all have been at this moment: December 31, 1999, 11:59:59 to January 1, 2000, 12:00:01, if it weren't for Y2K?

And this whole Y2K industry, spawned in those last few years of The Second Millennium. Well-paying, yet short-lived.

Fear is the trump card. The Millennium is coming. Fear monetized "I don't know" in telling us we don't know what is on the other side. "I don't know" became authoritative.

Insight, character, real leadership, these took a back seat. Traits in men like Egan, these were needed in this decade.

I bet you didn't know that our nation's military academies—Annapolis, West Point, Colorado Springs, New London—outlawed "I don't know."

At these places, "I'll find out" is the correct way to say "I don't know."

During an international crisis, would you want your military leaders' answer to be "I don't know" or "I'll find out"?

The First Decade of The Third Millennium killed I'll Find Out.

In The Information Age, it's all about fear and ignorance.

What caused The Great Recession? I don't know.

Fear, dressed in a grey suit and yellow tie, turns to the camera from behind the news desk and in that oh-so-newslike-voice says, "The Fear Index is holding steady. Volatility is implied. Stay tuned." No. "Stay... tuned..."

This isn't just another New Year's Eve.

The very nanosecond we crossed from one millennium to another, this was A New Nanosecond of A New Millisecond of A New Second of A New Minute of A New Day of A New Week of A New Month of A New Year of A New Decade of A New Century of A New Millennium.

Fear was offering to buy the crew the next round of shots. If the ability to buy shots still exists in a few seconds...

Or maybe you were drunk *and* high. Your dealer came through. Know what? Fuuuuuck you.

Waking up that next morning, on your buddy's laundry room cement floor. The First Morning of The First Day of The First Century of The Third Millennium.

Rolling over, knee hitting the dryer. You are here—no—you're *still* here. On this Earth.

For now...

Pulling all funds out of those financial institutions two days before, them trying to talk you out of it. But the looks in the employees' eyes told you they pulled their money out, too.

Now from your buddy's floor, looking around at the world.

Getting your bearings, setting the X- and Y-axis for this new millennium.

A few months from now, could be huddling in some drainage ditch, humming "Auld Lang Syne" in fits of half-sanity to keep spirits high. Raising an imaginary plastic champagne glass, hugging the vision of those friends as you all dine on raw rat meat.

Rawratmeat. Yumyumyum.

Those friends who got eaten by that crazed horde of Y2K-infected barbarian sex cannibals after the horde tired of having their way with them.

This decade, you didn't know so much about it back then. Not like you know now, now that you're older.

You didn't yet know any of those things that happened during those ten years that spurred you to name this decade The I Don't Know Decade.

Though you did know that the coke dealer didn't show up that previous night.

Fear bought a lot of rounds of shots, you knew that, too.

The Fear Index, you might have known what that was, don't remember. It wasn't optioned back then, so no way you could have known that people would one day speculate on futures of fear.

Egan? He was just some rising star back then. This was maybe when he got Stevie ran out, then got promoted.

Stevie was the quietest person in the room, who would open his mouth for like two sentences in the middle of a discussion and *floor* the room with insight. An angle, a perspective on the issue that would open up new avenues. Sharon was like that, too, only not as quiet as Stevie.

People like that made talentless corporate suck-ups like Egan shit. And Sharon, being both more talkative than Stevie *and* female, that creates whole new dimensions of negativity with guys like Egan.

Back to this moment, 1/1/00: the crazy thing is, with everything Y2K was bringing, all the potential scenarios for destruction, airliners were still just airliners back then. They took off and landed. That was it. It was a great idea to buy a house back then. Layoffs didn't happen back then like they do now.

New Orleans, Florida, islands in The Indian Ocean, they were different back then. Family members were alive back then.

We weren't involved in two different wars back then.

Our men and women in uniform weren't being wounded and killed on a daily basis back then.

You didn't read the word "fear" in the news as much as you do now back then.

Implied volatility. Y2K.

Know what? Time to say it. One of us has to.

Thanks, granddads and great-granddads. Thanks a lot.

Y2K: that whole "inputting the whole year" thing was really hard, wasn't it?

"Gee, which would be better to put in for the date on these machines: two numbers or four?"

"Duuuh, I don't know."

Dumbshit jack-nozzles.

One more time: how much more starry-eyed would we all have been if it weren't for Y2K?

6

Each day the economic news only gets worse. Even if it improves, it still feels like it's getting worse. If not, somebody discovers the angle that makes it worse.

That negativity, guys like Egan turned that into a managerial tool.

Egan.

Egan is in the lake, how many days now? Fish food.

Well, Egan *was* fish food.

Then fish shit. Fish *do* shit, right?

Egan, fish food. Egan fish food.

The Egan brand of fish food. Egan Fish Food™.

Package up that name, and actually put it to work, real work. Not that idiotic mutation of the school playground politics disguised as work that carried that guy through his life.

Egan Fish Food™. Registration mark pending.

Tap into the climate, that vibe in the air.

Egan Fish Food™ would be punishment food. Keep-fish-in-line food. Intimidating fish food. Bring-out-the-worst-in-fish fish food. Keep-them-on-their—wait, fish don't have toes.

Destroy-spirit-and-hope-and-ambition food.

Fish pee on the carpet again? Egan Fish Food™! Wait, fish don't pee on carpets.

Egan Fish Food™ gets fish back in line quicker than a cattle prod.

Fish will fear Egan Fish Food™.

Registration mark pending.

Egan Fish Food™ will train and condition fish. Talk about a niche. Tell me this has been thought of before. Disciplinary fish food. Trademark this fucker.

No more spending your child's college money on ceramic castles and sunken ceramic pirate ships for their aquariums. Over the course of time, if you do this right, Mister or Missus Fish Owner, all you'll need to do is pull the box of Egan Fish Food™ out of the cupboard, give it a few shakes. And registration mark is pending.

Fish will fear Egan Disciplinary Fish Food™.

Some type of million-dollar idea exists. It's time to corner the disciplinary fish food market.

Registration mark is no longer pending.

Time for the Egan® brand of fish food to upend the business world. Cause a bit of trouble.

I apologize for the unnecessary pain due to the fact that I know so little about hammer-purchasing. It was my first time.

But gotta admit it: Egan® is fucking interesting. You may not agree, but I haven't been this inspired in quite a while.

Back to this: Egan® Disciplinary Fish Food, muthafucka. A brand based on your life.

We'll even hire a graphic designer to do up your name into some cool logo. A logo much cooler than you could have ever aspired to be, back when you were—

Dude. What up?

Your final moments of life, the back bedroom, you should have seen yourself.

And now, Egan, here you are. You are here. I am pants-shitty.

Haunt. A cousin of Fear.

Egan: did I—WAITWAITWAIT—

Check it out. This is my impression of Egan and St. Peter, at The Pearly Gates.

Saint Peter: "And your name is?"

Egan: "Egan."

Saint Peter: "Wait. Aren't you that woman-hating homophobe who used any costume-related function to cross-dress and get *way* too into your feminine side? Like when Stevie had that trailer trash party years ago, you were just a supervisor then. You showed up all slutted out in a mini-skirt and heavy makeup with fake bruises, begging everyone to beat your 'whiskey-tango ass'?"

"Yeah?"

"Son, Heaven welcomes octillions upon octillions of souls, and we try not to judge up Here, but that was just plain creepy. And we're not even beginning to address how you assumed control of the CompReCam initiative in '06 and ran that project into the ground then covered your tracks by justifying laying off the project's three originators. We have a giant list of things here..."

7

Haunt. A cousin of Fear.

Egan needs to get to Heaven.

And someone needs to call the camp counselors and tell them to update what the kids tell each other by those campfires. The Civil War Dead, women who were unfairly tried then executed as witches, and headless horsemen are a thing of the past.

Hateful white guys who harass interns and drive Department Q-Drex scores down by 14.2% are taking over the ghost stories.

Egan, I may be out of line, but know what? Now you are justifying your existence in ways you never fathomed existed back when you actually existed. Before: justifying your existence consumed you, guided your path.

Now this justification flows before you. I'm seeing this as the first step to impressing the Heavens. Totally different vibe you're giving off here, the haunting me/ghost guy thing.

The Chairman of The Board of The Board of Boards meant for this to happen. Whatever is done with Egan®, your part is set in stone. I mean first off, there's the company name. Duh.

In life, you trucked with Fear. In death, you ride with Haunt. That façade, your old façade, you should have let go of that façade because—

If you indeed cared about your survival and your kids more than that façade you called your life and that image you pushed onto the world, you would have admitted that your ego wasn't nearly as important as your life and that fear was not only a smokescreen but your crutch, that you were—

But you didn't, which disappointed me to no end. But now here you are, haunting me.

Not only are we launching Egan®. We're using that Egan® money to buy back your soul, Egan. Yup.

That's my duty, I get it. They probably have you on some type of probationary period, like a conditional hire. They looked at everything you did in life and aren't quite sold yet.

How ever many people you had laid off or run out, Egan® will employ that many people. There we go, that'll get the Heavens excited about you, dude.

Egan destroyed jobs. Egan® creates jobs.

Jobs are the key to buying back your soul. Git some, my friend. After everything I did, you still came to me for help. I'm honored. I have a soul to help buy back and payrolls to make, I will give this endeavor my everything.

Most companies are all about profits for profits' sake. Egan® has an objective based in the universal planes of existence far beyond this Earth. Buying back a soul, what could be more noble than that?

Soul buyback and employing people to make up for laying off people, this is new capitalistic territory Egan® is trailblazing.

I can see you up there, standing in front of Them with that entitled smirk on your face, and once They started to read off your list of transgressions that smirk started to whither away. The powers that be, Them, giving you grief about everything you did in life. Now you're here and you need a hand to spiffen up your image. Gladly, my friend, gladly.

You returned to Earth calling in a favor to me, this is like some Mafia thing—well, kind of a Mafia thing (no wait, actually this really isn't like a Mafia thing).

Still: you're calling in that favor from the one person who is obligated more than anyone. And Egan: yes, I understand what is expected of me.

I'm no killer. And I get that look. Yes, I could have come to this realization a while ago. How right you are.

But it will be my honor to do everything in my power to help Egan buy back his soul. This will be my attempt at repairing the damage related to choosing a tack hammer instead of a thirteen-ounce Light Duty. It is now time to help you buy—

Whooaaaaa what was I thinking?

That's a great one and all, buying back your soul, but here's how I'm going to sweeten this deal. Egan: to further show you that that Hammer Death Beating Guy isn't the real me, and besides that, we're not thinking big enough here and I need to show you the kind of guy I really am.

Here it goes: I'm sending your kids to college, motherfucker.

After we successfully launch Egan®, and in five to ten years when we sell it for millions, each of your kids. College funds. Even the third one you didn't sell to an A-rab or some Chink.

Bartender, a round of college funds for Egan's three unwanted children.

Egan's soul. Jobs. College funds. This company has some work to do.

Now. As you're crystallizing, the reason why you reappeared is crystallizing. And, at the very least, I should admit some things to you.

First off: dude, I panicked. That's why you, as your soul left your body, looked the way you did.

Remember: I was using a tack hammer, swinging it with all I had. I wanted this to end, too. I could have walked away, and let you fade out, in pain. But I'd have a hard time living with myself afterward. I panicked.

Panic. Fear's maternal twin. Fear and Panic. Fear is dull. Panic is exciting. While Fear exists for the long-term, Panic is a firefly, living only for a short length of time. Panic panics because Panic can't convey its excitement about the world to the world.

Panic died two minutes after Panic and Fear were born because in a moment of panic, all rationality shut down and Panic decided to kill itself.

Fear has Panic's body cryo-frozen. From infancy onward, Fear's scientific endeavor has been to resurrect Fear's twin, Panic.

Panic, Baby Nicky.

Trippy shit.

You succeeded in life by harnessing the power of fear. You made me panic in your final moments of life. And now you're haunting me, Egan.

I've had stupid ideas before, but this one, WOW. If I only knew this uncertainty now, back then, when I was younger. Will these festering feelings lead to misery? I was ignorant and doubtful when it comes to ending another human being's life. I panicked.

I've come to a realization, Egan. And I'm happy that you're the first soul to hear me say what I'm about to say.

Egan: I suck at killing people. I'll say it again, dude. My forte is NOT killing people.

And for a flash there, I thought you were just going to be the first of many incompetent executives—WHOOPS was I wrong.

It's time to hang up my hammer.

I got some college funds to pay for and a soul to buy back and people to employ so they can finance their own dreams and a cross to bear and an industry to create.

8

"The Fear Index is fluctuating wildly," Fear says, looking into the camera from behind the news desk. "The Misery Index is threatening to stomp on the world's throat. Unpaid Overtimers are still receiving e-mails full of dotdotdots but no actual actionable information. The Shit-Fucking Dance is at an all-time high, and the feelings of Job Suck-Curity are skyrocketing. That's the news and goodnight."

Your old room, this is good. In the previous decade we'd be thinking loft space downtown and hip furniture and cool art for the walls to show the world that Egan® is serious when it comes to disciplinary fish food.

But in this decade, you show the world you don't fuck around by *not* buying all that shit. Converting a room of a house into a business to save money and focus on the launch, that's how Egan® gets it done.

I'll have to measure the square footage of this space for tax purposes.

Egan® will be a post-Great Recession type of business and generator of revenue.

Speaking of money, yup, I did it. We're starting a new industry here. Disciplinary fish food needs to launch with a bang. So I cashed out my retirement money. It was vicious. I'm paying more than 40 percent in penalties and have to pay taxes on it.

But we got investment capital.

Taking my retirement money to the bank was pretty cool. There's this teller. I like the look on her face, she doesn't seem to be freaking about this recession and hopped-up-on-fear world. Always has this smile. Lunch hour, making that bank run used to be the best part of my day at the old office sometimes.

Today I said just put that puppy in with my checking. Good thing you never saw her when you were alive, you would've said something and then I would have hit you and gotten fired.

Yeah, you're right. I was too chickenshit to hit you back then.

I also set up an account at the overnight delivery place. They have a notary. These days it's all about covering your ass.

And you *are* cool with me converting your old room into the office, right?

Yeah, now my mortgage is suddenly an issue and the investment capital isn't what it should be so I can't quit the old job yet so goodbye nights and weekends, but man, risk feels good.

Besides, those narcissistic bank autojerkoffs got bailed out by the taxpayer and now aren't lending because they're too busy falling in love with themselves. Hey banks: disciplinary fish food. Pull up your pants and get back to work.

As much as I'd love to quit and be here full time, I still gotta work the other job for at least a while, be all sneaky-like, use their supplies to keep our costs low, but call this back bedroom The Egan® Disciplinary Fish Food Worldwide—no fuck that—UNIVERSEWIDE Headquarters, Incorporated, Inc.

This company is about checking your egos at the door, rolling up your sleeves, and figuring out how to communicate to the world that their current fish food may not command the respect of your fish like you thought it did.

Got that Customer Meeting/Pow-Wow table at some secondhand sale. Moved my desk in here. The corkboards on the walls, imagine those walls not long from now. Ideas about distribution, production schedules, marketing, negotiation strategies, short- and long-term disciplinary fish food trends, cross-partnerships, line extensions, financial forecasts, celebrity endorsement/disciplinary fish food ideas—all littering the walls.

I also had a cool idea. Not like it applies to you since you can't meet with them, but I figure until we get Egan® to a farther place, I can just have my disciplinary fish food meetings with various people involved in the enterprise at coffee houses or whatever. I'll shoot for before work, at lunch, or happy hours—DAMN I love these corkboard walls.

We need to figure out how to do business differently, the last few years have taught us that. And I don't think a business has ever been started with the express intent of saving souls through capitalism.

Look at those walls. Maybe one day, one brainfart gets scribbled down and tacked up there, then weeks later one of us sees it and has an idea and we take this random brainfart and turn it into a solution and suddenly, BOOM, we've removed another hurdle from the Egan® launch.

The subconscious mind is an amazing thing.

The Egan® brand is going to be a success because of our optimism and freedom to think of ideas. No holding back, no fear. Like in your old life, that intimidation, all that corporate bullshit, won't fly here.

You're right. I shouldn't bring that up, you're right.

The past is the past. Back to Egan®. We have your kids' college educations and your soul to think about.

Again: no idea is a bad idea within this space, Egan.

Okay. No idea *except* tack hammer death beatings.

Enough fucking around. Let's go to work. Go-To-Market. The Egan® Go-To-Market Strategy.

First thing's first, thought of this last night before going to bed. This is how we look at Egan®, going forward:

Fuck sex. Fear is what sells.

That's our company mantra in making Egan® a success in the marketplace. Think souls and college educations. Fuck sex. Fear is what sells. That's how Egan® does things.

In Marketing they spend many hours concocting stories and lore about these entities called brands. A brand is an attempt to humanize an inanimate object or service. The idea being to manufacture an emotional connection with a potential buyer.

Fish food, fish food, fish food—discipline-inducing fish food.

Idea: "Never fear! Egan® is here!"

"Panicky? Uncertain? Doubtful? Ignorant? Miserable? Stock up on Egan®."

Registration mark is no longer pending. Sweet Jesus is it no longer pending.

We're gonna need a logo sooner or later. The Positioning Statement, the stake in the ground. This is Egan®. Got some college tuitions to pay for and souls to buy back.

Slogan thoughts:

Egan® Fish Food: Your fish will almost feel satisfied.™

Egan®: It's practically satisfying.™

Egan® Fish Food reinforces to the fish that they are not worthy of complete satisfaction. Once this point is driven home, your fish will crawl into the corner and cry little fish tears.

Wait—is Government Order #1497823 still in effect? Banning fish from hanging out on land?

Back to work. Imagine the best steak dinner ever.

Start off with escargot for an appetizer. Garlic. Butter. Sizzle. Dry martini, three olives.

Next, they bring that iceberg lettuce wedge. The bleu cheese in the dressing has been aged longer. The chef improvised with added hints of paprika and cinnamon. These balance nicely—and applewood-smoked bacon bits were fried up specifically for this plate. Bacon is an easy ingredient to pre-cook, but remember:

We're imagining the best steak dinner you've ever had. We're all about freshly cooked bacon bits.

And now, the main attraction—excuse me—the main course.

A dry aged New York strip steak. Aged twenty-one days. So tender. Sunday-afternoon-laying-in-bed-shooting-the-breeze-with-women-who-no-longer-speak-to-you tender.

Medium rare. The ideal temperature for a steak this tender.

One end is propped up on the side of saffron, garden-fresh rosemary and thyme, garlic-infused mashed potatoes, and lightly topped with diced fresh mint leaves. A mix of flavors you'd never imagine to infuse so well.

The potatoes are made with real butter. Our world has gotten to a point where this point needs to be stated.

The sautéed spinach, Brussels sprouts, mushrooms, and red pepper round out the dish. These were seared in a pan at high heat with diced baby onions and scallions and reduced with white wine. But the star of this show is the steak.

The Cabarnet was chosen because it's a lighter Cabarnet. Again, it will complement and round out the steak, not compete with it.

You carve out the first bite.

If your ideal meal wasn't this, that's cool.

Dig in. Enjoy.

Now it's time to push your plate away. One more bite is literally impossible at this point.

Dessert? Maybe that's a part of your ideal meal. Not mine.

Anyway, fear, the Egan® core brand equity, now tells you to remove 15 percent of this full feeling.

All of that goodness, remove 15 percent of it. And remember: you can't take another bite.

You don't deserve it, this last 15 percent. You deserve to be 85 percent satisfied. Quit thinking about that other 15 percent, you selfish sack of shit.

Egan® Disciplinary Fish Food will leave your fish 85 percent satisfied.

Right where you want them.

Egan® will make your fish feel alive. Somewhat.

The meal itself looked like it was going to leave them 115 percent satisfied. But that's the magical talent of fear. And after a while, this unworthiness feeling builds and down the road even that 85 percent feels like it is too much.

In the middle of all of this is the essence of Egan®. Leverage fear.

Gonna leverage some capital for some souls, oh hell yes.

The key is to get them hooked, hooked on chasing that 100 percent, then after time, that 85 percent.

Figure this out, sell Egan® off to some gigantic corporation years from now and make some muhhhh-fuckin' money. We gettin' paid.

Look out college: Egan's kids are coming.

Let these fish think that this last 15 percent is achievable. They're fish. Fuck 'em. Guard this truth. Give them a clear picture of pure satisfaction.

Satisfaction. Only a picture, go ahead and frame it. Why not?

Why lead them and inspire them to greatness, to go above-and-beyond? Feed them Egan® Fish Food instead.

Egan, this is a start, but I don't think fear is enough to go on here for the Egan® brand.

Egan® needs more. Fear is the centerpiece of what we need to leverage, but we need more.

"More" equals souls and college educations.

9

Misery.

Egan® needs to leverage misery, with slight hints of ruthlessness, relentlessness, and remorselessness.

Remember, Egan: we're not selling to fish here, but fish owners. They are overworked and trying to keep it together here in this new decade, only the craziness is still pouring in from the last one. They need to know that Egan® leverages effective amounts of misery keeping their fish in line.

We need to create some type of graphic on the packaging, The Misery Index™. No, that's that financial-thingie, so we have to call it The Egan® Misery Index, so the lawyers won't sue us.

But yeah, some little graphic of an index—no, an official-looking seal, like a crest—on the fish food box, says, "Meets required Misery Index standards, .0001MG: Ruthlessness/Relentlessness/Remorselessness" or whatever.

Fear needs a Gestapo, dedicated to fostering misery. Fear's Head of Gestapo is Monsieur E. Monsieur E is miserable and small. Seven foot ten inches tall. Miserable, sadistic. Fear, channeling misery for torture.

The Less Triplets—Ruth, Relent and Remorse—are ruthless, relentless, and remorseless in running The Secret Police at Monsieur E's side. Six-foot-one. Too sadistic to strut the runways, though each could land a modeling contract if they were human.

Misery. The Misery Index. Yeah, I know it's bullshit, but this is that Marketing part of this. It's bullshit, but not bullshit. Put a tiny graphic on the packaging. Some type of government-looking seal. Subtle. It'll look more official that way, which is what we want.

Speaking of what we want, we want a copy strategy. The copy strategy is the words and phrases we'll use to market to people, the slogans we'll put in advertisements and on the website and teach to the future salesforce. Like "85% Satisfying," like that. Wait.

Our copy strategy is all about doubt.

Egan® and its copy strategy need to create doubt in fish owners' heads about the validity of their current fish food. Yes, Egan® needs to own doubt.

"Your fish will ravenously enjoy Egan® Fish Food, yet doubt their inner selves for enjoying it." Some selling premise like that. That's a good start for a thought, though.

We spur Egan® trial by getting these overworked Unpaid Overtimers to doubt their current fish food.

Doubt.

Little Miss Doubt is the loving younger sister of Fear and Baby Nicky. Four-foot-eleven yet so not four-foot-eleven. Curvy, round butt you want to nibble on.

Little Miss Doubt melds sultry with cutesy, casually referencing previous boyfriends and men that she thinks are hot. Your rational, intelligent self knows not to take her comments seriously, but you do.

Don't get her wrong... You're good and all...

Egan, doubt is all about—dude. DUDE.

The Egan® Copy Strategy is all about the doubt-inducing ellipses.

Dotdotdot.

"Is your current fish food doing the job..."

Unpaid Overtimer, is your current fish food doing the jobDOTDOTDOT.

Ellipses points, brilliant.

Egan: our consumer receives these dotdotdots on a day-in/day-out basis. They're bombarded—no, chicken-shit sniper-bulleted—by them. Friday afternoon, they're getting ready to head out for the weekend, can't wait to get to buy some fish food, and dotdotdot they get that last e-mail from the boss...

"Monday…Let's talk, re…Simpson Q4 project…"
DOTDOTDOT
Right before heading out for the weekend, to the fish food store, this e-mail infuses doubt into their weekend.

And there we are, Egan®, big old disciplinary fish food box and its Misery Index on some billboard or flashing sign as they're driving to the fish food store, interrupting them thinking about the Simpson Q4 project…—and WHAMMO. The Egan® brand is saying something about "Is your current fish food doing the job…"

Ellipses. Dotdotdot. They just saw these ellipses in the e-mail, now they're filled with doubt, and BOOM, we're getting them to doubt their current brand of fish food.

We create enough doubt, Egan, guess what?

Payrolls are made. Your soul is bought. Your kids are going to college. Boo-yah.

Ellipses. Yes. You notice ellipses, they are just like sniper bullets. They come out of nowhere.

…

See?

What a valuable element to have in our copy strategy, ellipses points.

But Egan, let's think. Egan®.

Our target is Unpaid Overtimers, right? Egan® needs to reach these people, connect with them. Understand their uncertainty.

With the job, housing market, the economy, these Unpaid Overtimers have learned to live with the IDK Decade brand of uncertainty. September 11, Iraq, Internet and housing bubbles, vanishing retirement funds, global outsourcing, Katrina, The Tsunami, years of war and our soldiers dying—then the economic crash in 2008, afterward, IDK took it out of these people. Egan® knows that.

It's like it almost started in 2000, when we held an election, yet failed to elect a President.

After Y2K, what better way to keep the uncertainty ball rolling than to hold an election yet not elect a President eleven months later?

For a span of time, from November 7, 2000 to December 13, 2000, the future was uncertain. This was the first time ever in America that this happened.

The race so close, so much uncertainty.

If we figure out how to tap into this uncertainty, Egan® is off and running.

UncertainTina is Fear's favorite whore. And wife. Fear has many whores and hires and fires many, but UncertainTina is always there. She was beautiful once. The blonde hair is still radiant. Those millennia of hard drugs took their toll on her looks but still, you would. Wouldn't be boring.

Fear and UncertainTina.

Egan, this uncertainty thing, there with the fear thing, it's cool. But we need a fish food element to it, too. Something to keep the uncertainty vibe going—Here you go: each piece of fish food looks the same, only we have different flavors inside. So as they're biting into it, fish are filled with uncertainty regarding flavor. One bite is raspberry, the next is salted margarita. This will keep them on their—wait, fish don't have toes.

Still.

This is part of the Disciplinary Fish Food Selling Premise: "Egan® will keep fish uncertain and on their 'toes.'"

Biting into each new fish food piece, they won't know what to expect. Forever on their "toes."

Their owners live with uncertainty, so they need to live with uncertainty.

Egan®. Fish food. Misery, doubt, uncertainty—

Ignorance. Egan® Disciplinary Fish Food needs to capitalize upon ignorance.

That I Don't Know Decade brand of ignorance. Here you go: it's like company cultures that strive to keep employees ignorant of the outside world, almost like third-world dictatorships. If we can communicate to our consumers that Egan® understands that brand of ignorance and is all about keeping their fish ignorant of other opportunities, this fact will resonate with them, Egan.

Here's the magic formula: fear and ignorance equals college funds and souls.

Ignorance.

Doctor Igno Rance is Fear's Minister of Propaganda.

Thin and wiry, with glasses. Works behind the scenes. Don't let the soft-spoken voice fool you. One needs to be sadistic to do this job.

Monsieur E is Fear's Head of Secret Police. Doctor Igno is Fear's Propaganda Czar. Their common goal is to foster living in fear. They hate each other.

Yes, this ignorance, this energy. Egan® needs that IDK ignorance in its marketing. Maybe part of the sales story—Here you go: in The Information Age, everyone seems to get more and more ignorant. Know what brand of fish food understands that? Egan®.

Maybe Egan® Fish Food contains a motivating agent, based in memory or lack thereof. No, work. We fear work. Old-fashioned view of hard work paying off has been distorted the last ten years. More work less reward more thankful for this lessened reward.

This is prime Egan® marketing territory.

Our target needs to compensate. Egan® is about artificially filling the leadership gap. What a great substitute for big-mindedness, compassion, inspiration, drive, character.

Every day, in the office, in our world, doubt, ignorance, misery, panic, uncertainty—our daily fearmongering. Who understands? What brand understands them?

Egan®.

Once we start building a sales team, we'll figure out some sales tactics based on ignorance, doubt, uncertainty—

Idea: back to that steak vibe we had a while ago:

Steak-flavored disciplinary fish food.

If you say *that* has been thought of before, you can fuck right off.

What? *What?*

The steak idea: fish do eat steak, right?

Need to research fish food and figure out what fish actually do eat.

Regardless though, the Egan® Go-To-Market Strategy: misery, doubt, uncertainty, ignorance, along with fear and panic, ruthlessness, relentlessness, and remorselessness. Definitely assets we can capitalize upon. I'm feeling good.

But we really should learn what fish do in fact actually eat before proceeding further.

10

"A newly laid-off father of five shot his wife and children to death today then committed suicide. Just in time for Ratings Week."

Fear is dressed in a grey suit, sky blue shirt, paisley tie. Fear's hair is a bit longer, styled into a sweep of the bangs. From behind the news desk, Fear shuffles papers and looks into the camera.

"Also, The Fear Index is out of hand, but you knew that. In other news, www.werethoseventurecapitalistshighonmethwhentheyfundedou rpieceofshitwebsite.com, www.weareaninternetcompanythereforewea reautomaticallygoingtomakemillions.com, www.businessplan?whyhavea businessplanwhenwehaveawebsite.com, www.esotericnonsensicalname thathasnothingtodowiththeproductorservice.com all went under. And guess what? Your stock options are worthless. WORTHLESS. Tune in later.

Your stock options, being pissed on. Film at 11.

And now let's cut to the factory floor at a car manufacturer in Michigan, where that tiny slut sis o' mine, Little Miss Doubt, is on location."

The camera cuts to Little Miss Doubt, dressed in a black business suit, two too many buttons on the white shirt are open, blonde hair in a bun. Bright red lipstick. She's at the car factory.

"A car company in Detroit unveiled The Pollutionator™ today. It's an SUV the size of a one-story house."

She and the camera crew slowly walk around The Pollutionator™ while Little Miss Doubt shows it all off for the camera. Her curves slide along the vehicle's curves. She holds the microphone with one hand, while slowly running the fingernails of her other hand across the different features of The Pollutionator™.

She walks down from the SUV's sun porch and closes with "It gets eighteen feet to the gallon. This is Little Miss Doubt reporting, back to you, Fear."

Cut back to Fear at the news desk. Doctor Igno is sitting next to Fear in the guest commentator chair, dark suit and shirt, dark tie, horn-rimmed glasses. Fear speaks into the camera. "Thanks for pumping up the sluttitude, little sis. This *is* Ratings Week. Doctor Igno Rance is here to bring all of us up-to-date on that horrible, awful, unspeakable tragedy unfolding at Enron. Doctor Igno."

"Thank you for having me, Fear. Some traders at Enron were caught on tape bragging about their manipulation of California natural gas prices. Several widespread blackouts occurred during heatwaves. During one outage, Enron told California that they bumped the going rate to roughly $1400 per megawatt-hour from the forty- to fifty-dollar per megawatt-hour range one year earlier. In the aftermath of Enron's bankruptcy, executives exited the company with more than a billion dollars while rank-and-file employees lost their pensions. During the heatwave in which they intentionally inflated prices, people died.

But Fear, what's truly compelling is that Enron somehow timed this story to hit during Ratings Week. Already, Corporate is showing positive gains."

"It's uncanny, Doctor Igno, their impeccable sense of timing. You'd think all the rich white guys are in cahoots or something. And please keep us up to date—What is that?"

Fear turns away from Doctor Igno and says that last part as he puts his hand up to his earpiece, "Go ahead. Okay." Fear turns to speak directly into the camera.

"Folks, we have a quick update from Monsieur E, who is in the Arctic Circle after Vice President Cheney just issued his National Energy Plan."

The news cuts to Monsieur E, sitting on a rock by a daytime campfire in the Arctic, melting glaciers in the background, chunks of ice falling into the water. A polar bear carcass is slowly spinning on the spit over the fire.

Monsieur E, all almost eight feet of him, dominates the screen. Monsieur E is gnawing on a polar bear rib, bits of flesh and gristle line the mouth. He looks around, occasionally into the camera lens. Sunlight bounces off both the snow and Monsieur E's bald head.

Fear says, "Monsieur E, hello? Can you hear us out there?"

The microphone clipped to the black leather trench coat captures Monsieur E's every chew and digestive sound and grunt and burp. This goes on for ten seconds, then the camera cuts back to Fear.

"Monsieur E, hello? Damn satellite feed. We'll try again later in the broadcast. In the meantime folks, let's talk real estate."

As Fear starts to talk real estate, the camera pans over to the studio's open stage, to the right of the news desk, where each of the Less Triplets strikes a slow pose while holding an oversized presentation graphic card portraying a different negative real estate trend.

Each is wearing a conservative-cut blue business suit. After a few seconds, you realize the suits are body paint, not cloth. The five-inch heels are real, though.

Once Fear is finishing talking real estate, Fear says, "…and to re-cap: that was the real estate market. Thanks to our market analysts Ruth Less, Relent Less, and Remorse Less, the Less Triplets. And folks: don't miss our upcoming investigative news special, 'The Y2K-Infected Barbarian Sex Cannibals: Was 1/1/00 Just Their Smokescreen?', hosted by my crank-whore of a wife, UncertainTina. Though do keep an eye on scheduling. She might end up going on a last-minute shopping spree and/or crystal meth/pill binge.

And before we go further, one being that hasn't been mentioned yet is Sivvie, my apprehensively apprehensive Man-Assistant. Call Sivvie the Patron Saint of Job Suck-Curity. We don't mention Sivvie much because we don't give a fuck about Sivvie. Wait." Fear starts to giggle. "Hang on. Sivvie! Get in here!"

Sivvie, tall and skinny, apprehensively steps into view by the desk, looking into the camera. Fear face-punches Sivvie as hard as Fear can, and the viewer can hear laughter from off-camera as Sivvie sheepishly walks off the set. "Job Suck-Curity" is heard a few times, along with the snickers.

Back to Fear, who is shaking that fist.

"And unfortunately we have to cut this newscast short this evening. My newly-resurrected panicky twin brother Baby Nicky was going to deliver the weather report for late summer 2001, but unfortunately the little zombie-toddler had a panic attack and diaper-shit itself."

II

Dont change the channel

Fear's big br,other Terror is dominating the airwaves and Tv Screens

When Terror strikes punctuation and spacing Terror says fuckthat are Any typos you see well you see how to explainTerrorjustsay Terror

Th copyedittors apologizeTerror showed up

Its c'ool.We get it.You say.We getTerror

Terror look over ther e Terror andthere

Terror

When Little Miss Doubt Baby Nicky and Fear's big brother Terror showed up

Terror doesn't just destroy people and buildings and airplanes it

Oh look you tried to change the channel but Terror dominates this channel too

Back to the subjec

Invites itself into your life only whn Terror invit.es itself into yo ur life,, you don't have a choice inthe matter

Terror is a gigantic part of yo:ur life after it first strikes Terror becomes like a family

Oh look you logged on to a website to escapeyouwerethinking it wouldn"t be aboutTerror but it's aboutTerror toughshit gofuckyourself and dealwithwhatyou'reseeing back to the subject let's talk about it on ths website versus TV, fine,Terror isnn' picky, choose your medium, Terror is mult-imedia back to conversation

Member when Terror shows up on beautiful cloudless days
Terror takes over your life Terror says get used to it
In those first visceral moments after your introduction to Terror
You can't" take your mind off Terror One thing before we go further fear uncertainty misery doubt panic and ignorance may be valuable brand equities to leverage in launching and marketing a product

But terror will never be an element of a brand"s character or go-to market strategy at least it shouldn't never damn well should our world is pretty fucking messed up as it is imagine if we started leveraging terror to sell products

And Terrror wants every manager who ever brags about usng Fear that little brother of his to manage that each and every one of you are weak reall leaders know how to lead quitt walking aroundd like fear is a managerial trrait

Step it up a notch, fearmonger. If you had a spine you would terror-monger, Fear's big brother wouldsay.

Back to Other ThOughtthink about it again: Imagine if we started leveraging terror to sell products

Something else to know

After this chapter you will not read the words Terror or terror in this book again we might talk about terrrorrelated events cant help it but the wrod terror won't appear again

But Terror will be there

50 pages from now Terror will be there

As you read this book's last word Terror will be there

Fear's big brother only gives a shit about you when you are visceral

When you are visceral you are Terror's whole universe

Visceral is what Terror devours torches basks in

Over time visceral burns out its visceral and short term and is fleeting

When you are no longer visceral you no longer matter Terror no longer cares at the same time typos don't appear as often and spacing realigns normalcy returns somewhat you start to make sense of things and gain perspective

When this happens, Terror is off to another universe

Fear, Little Miss Doubt and Baby Nicky's big brother takes off NO hurtles off

For a flash of time, you were visceral

That flash of time, Terror ferociously ecstatically loves visceral

Guess what?

The concept of visceral is just like the concept of a chapter in a book.

Sooner or later, both of them end.

12

I looked up fish food ingredients. We were waaay overthinking it.

We can do wheat, soybeans, or fish byproduct (what's left over after making tuna fish). Fish byproduct—cannibal fish. Y2K-Infected Barbarian Sex Cannibals. Time flies.

With Egan®, capitalizing on fear and that evolving brand of fear our consumers felt during that decade, I keep wondering if living in fear makes time go by quicker or slower. There was just something on about the Space Shuttle. That one exploded more than seven years now. Yeah, right?

2003. Flipping on the TV that Saturday morning, I first thought those were fireworks.

She doesn't speak to me any more. Many don't speak to me any more. Where was I going, the Space Shuttle, I remember thinking that living in fear was the norm. Anthrax, snipers, now this.

You live in fear. It was just a thought. Boom. Showed up in my head, matter-of-factlike.

After a visceral day that altered history forever, weeks turned into months then into years of dull misery, economic panic and uncertainty about both the macro and the micro, doubting politicians and ourselves, choosing ignorance over discovery. Living in fear.

The Space Shuttle exploding drove that point home.

The months since the layoff were miserable. Going in all day Sunday because management kept panicking, changing direction, avoiding logic, reminding…us…of…layoffs…I fought for that Saturday, though.

Got extra things done during the week, just be away for a full day in *mind* as well as body. Lounge with a cool chick, have a day before going in again on Sunday.

Plus, talk of a small layoff. This Saturday, let's not think about that.

It wasn't the amount of work, I loved working hard. It was the panic, doubt, fear, misery, uncertainty, and ignorance all disguised as work. Wait…Be…thankful…

WOW you all ratcheted up the fear. All you knew how to do was lead through fear. Leading by example is dead, isn't it?

That girl doesn't speak to me anymore.

White fireworks. Maybe the government saw the stress and threw a surprise Saturday morning fireworks show for the American worker. A fireworks display, like a surprise holiday for us. Our stress and overtime and no raise and picking up the slack, the government noticed and wanted to give us a quick escape. Fireworks.

To those that were stressing overtime and not getting paid for it because they didn't survive the layoff, this fireworks show is for you as well.

The TV sound was off because this bass-heavy club track was playing, volume low, must have been left in the CD player. Those fireworks mixing with the beat, the camera is unsteady and jumpy. Maybe shooting white comets, or some jets high up.

Cool fireworks, thanks Unpaid Overtimers. Wait—

FuckingChristdidthatguyinthesuitbehindthenewsdeskjustsaythatwas TheSpaceShuttle—

Columbia.

Egan, it was like the decade said, "Guess what, fuck-knocker? Here's some negative news about the space shuttle. You don't think about NASA a lot, but now even that train of thought is infused with fear. AND…Working tomorrow…is there a problem…"

My cousin out in Nebraska got laid off the week before. Me and the girl going into work that weekend. All three of us, Unpaid Overtimers.

Shut up. Those astronauts. Unpaid Overtimer: fuck your job shut the fuck up.

They cut to a shot of two of the astronauts' wives. That set the girl into tears.

A few weeks later, she told me how amazing I was that day. I can't remember what made me amazing, Egan.

We went for a walk, ate in silence at a place that served Bloody Marys. She cried about those astronauts' kids.

Reading positive news is like cheating on the negative news.

I wanted to be an astronaut when I was a kid. Early on, it was a bird. Then, a pterodactyl (dinosaur phase). Then, astronaut.

I bet those astronauts died without fear. Way more than possible, them being stronger than fear.

Enough memory lane. Egan, let's talk about the eight-hundred-pound gorilla in the room: why am I here during the workday, during the workweek, you ask?

I didn't take the day off, nope. I got fired.

What can I say? I bet they saw the gleam in my eye and got scared I might share all of this positivity with the other minions. Who cares? I was there all day wanting to be here, or I was falling asleep at my desk from working here all night.

Did I march out and make a scene, trying to convince my fellow co-workers to come with me and to see the fragile structure of fear-driven Corporate America for what it is?

Heck no, I let that magic carpet made of disciplinary fish food carry me out those doors. The disciplinary fish food even inspired a tune I hummed as they marched me out and I blew disciplinary fish food good-bye kisses to all of our former co-workers.

Though they did say I was professional and magnanimous in taking the lead on persuading everyone to sign the condolences card that Corporate sent to your family. They seemed to want to mention your name as quickly as possible then move on. That position they made up for you to get you out of the Corporate office, they're not looking for a replacement.

I guess I was in line for some promotion up until recently, too. But Egan, I took this firing as a sign.

We need disciplinary fish food equipment, we need to commission some disciplinary fish food studies, there's that fish food trade show we should attend—shit, we still need a logo. I can't ask you to provide. Duuuhhhh.

This *is* the worst economy since The Great Depression—whatever, you're right. It takes money to make disciplinary fish food.

That's why entrepreneurs are who they are, right?

I could have taken my dough and played Wall Street, buying and selling and trading and negotiating a bunch of Misery Indexes and Fear Indexes, but souls and college educations are expensive. Disciplinary fish food is the only way.

And as the saying goes, it takes money to make disciplinary fish food. I had to quit being the part-time partner. I caused all this and I was still pulling a paycheck.

So the Universe ordered me to jump out of a safe airplane, confident in that parachute made of disciplinary fish food strapped to my back.

I wasn't being fair to you, our souls, the Egan® employees, or your kids.

Dammit. We're slacking on the Go-To-Market document. See, it's good I got fired. The ships are burned. It's time to discover disciplinary fish food.

Another thing: fuck sex. Fear is what sells in this millennium.

13

Chairman of The Board of The Board of Boards:

It's no-longer-fear-God guy.

Yup, me.

I know you're done with me, and this has zero chance of changing, but know what? I'm speaking to You anyway, God.

It's a simple equation, God. You no longer hear me, I no longer fear You, so this is falling on deaf ears but get ready I'm gonna say my peace here goes. And by the way: I'm not even tempted to yell all this blasphemous stuff either to try to shock You into seeing me again, even though I no longer fear you. I could never do that.

I haven't been at work for five days, way behind with the tradeshow. Egan's gotta be pissed. And if some potential investor walked in, look at me. Wait, it's Saturday ni—Sunday morning. That'd be trippy if some investor—

Thank You, God, for the no-more-loud, thank you from the bottom of my heart. I hate the loud. I can't work with the loud, I need to work. Really, God, please understand what work is to me now. It's the only thing.

But since the loud stopped, what a positive angle it is on all of this, this business adventure. And with the business climate nowadays, every business needs all the good news it can get.

God, thank You for this insight as well. Such a positive angle. The negative commands so much attention but yes, the situation has a positive. God, I don't know if You are the one who lit up this positive but I'm going to believe You did.

My five-day absence, the radio silence, thanks to You, God, now I have a great way to look at it. Not gonna let me up there, the business down here I get it, thank you.

Thank you. The business goals are now significantly financially simplified, thus improving the chances of success.

Yes, in the midst of The Great Recession, this business now has an even bigger chance of making it than it did before thanks to this realization. What a different way to look at it. Forget the negative, be positive.

People's jobs and Egan's kids' college educations have been the only thing to worry about all along.

I hadn't looked into souls and their costs yet, but they can't be cheap. Removing that expense from the top-line—

And of course you know their costs, God, but freeing up Soulbuyback from our overhead costs, I just have to automatically assume that's a huge amount of money.

I was thinking, how about we go buy and sell a bunch of Misery and Fear Indexes for those kids' college educations? "I'll trade you ten Misery Indexes for seven Fear Indexes"—see, that's not hard. And the way things are going in this world, they're probably going to make Doubt Indexes, and Uncertainty, Panic, Igno—That would be so much easier.

No. You're right, God, I understand. Egan® is a real product, not some math equation. Egan® is the answer. Plus, it will employ people. And that money we were going to use on a soul—

I have to come clean here, God. I know You were on to me and didn't stop me. I don't know whether or not to thank You for that.

But here goes: that whole time, my desire to be part of helping my business partner/compadre's drive to buy back his soul. That sincerity and dedication, I was honored to be his silent partner.

I said Egan is a conditional hire, I get it. Those spotty things in his background, Heaven's HR people were hesitant to extend an offer, Egan® is his chance to prove himself, and he can't do it without me. I get it. No. I was honored.

I said, "If he needs to buy back his soul, then as a show of solidarity, I solemnly pledge that I need to buy back my soul," I said, "He was an underperforming FEARMONGERING FUCK IN LIFE"—shh, sorry, sorry—

And my agenda was he and I together focus on his soul and once You see everything he has done compared to that life he lived, maybe—

With his boy, he almost looked Dad-like, for a nanosecond.

Schobie's comment at lunch that day, years ago, after running into Egan over the weekend—

God: Egan's soul is 100 percent intact. I didn't do one thing to harm it. Every nanosecond of his life and afterlife, never once was Egan's soul in danger.

And mine is gone.

The magnitude of difference between what he did over the course of his life and what I did in a flash, it's crystal clear to me now.

Why he is where he is now versus where I'll be going, the circumstances behind all of this are crystal clear to me now.

Giving me an inkling of all that, that awful vision of where I'm going, now there's no way I can commit suicide. Very cunning of you.

I want to live forever. But only because I know where I'm going when I die.

All of my life I was taught to think of the Universe as a dangerous, unforgiving place that I need to fear. And now I know the truth. From the outside it's easy to appreciate what a loving and understanding place the Universe is, and why Egan was never in any danger. He may have to answer for some things, but not on any grand scale.

God: that night, his death, hammer issue aside, I was fine as rain. Loading him into the truck, getting out to the lake, no problem.

What Schobie said, 85 percent of him went through the wood chipper then I rememb—no—she said that, and it left my head until it returned out there by the lake when—

NO.

Here it is.

God: by the time everything progressed to the point it was when we were out by the lake, 85 percent of Egan's dead body was fed into that wood chipper by an inhuman no-longer-suicidal being who was coldly evaluating everything that seemed to deviate from the preconceived idea, in order to make the next kill more efficient.

Reduce headcount by 2000 in Q4 to excite Wall Street, as well as ignore the company's true problems. Kill incompetent executive and dispose of body in woodchipper due to woodchipper's rapid processing abilities.

The person who fed 85 percent of Egan into that hopper saw these two things as no different. If this is how the world is, then this is how it is.

That last 15 percent of Egan was placed into that thing a few hours later by a guy who saw every difference.

If this is how the world is, then this is how it is.

After Egan® sells and the college funds are set up, turning myself in is still on the table. But that's years down the road, I have a lot of work to do.

God, I sacrificed everything only to see fear for the pathetic force that it is. And that's a very good move You all pulled on me out there, giving me that faint glimpse of where I'm going, so now I can't kill myself.

I don't even know what I was allowed to know about my future, but it cuts off the suicide idea.

"Enjoy some decades, you'll appreciate these memories," The Inevitable said. "You'll never be able to love anyone again, but these memories you collect still will be valuable one day."

And notice that there weren't any ellipses in that, either. The Inevitable isn't some gutless fearmongering boss. It doesn't adopt some douche-smirk and say something like, "once you die, the real fun begins..." NO.

What am I doing? Why am I telling You what The Inevitable does? You're The Chairman of The Board of The Board of Boards.

I understand why crime sprees happen, the ones you read about and wonder how someone could inflict death and pain not just once but repeatedly.

When I was in 85 percent-land, it was in times like these, take a hammer to the status quo, this isn't personal.

And Egan made this easy, flying into town to tell Corporate his thoughts on headcount and office morale, being the new Senior District VP. They created that "Senior" position and relocated his family to get him out of Corporate. Mess up, get promoted. That's how it works.

He's the one who called me the week before, ordering me to "pick your old boss up at the hotel" that night and "chauffeur him to the titty bar." I was just beginning to plan this whole thing, his demand was good, now that I think about it. Planning was far enough along to bump up the timeline. And my original plan had more steps, this had a shorter timeline but the path was simplified.

He was half-drunk when I picked him up, waiting by the window in the lobby. Started on the plane, I guess. Just couldn't wait to get to the titty bar. This was good for tracing purposes, though, not having to call his phone. He just got in the car, I handed him the pint of whiskey/sleep aid which I was saving for later, he said, "Don't mind if I do, GODDAMN, kids are driving me NUTS!"

He was asleep halfway to my place. If I got stopped by a cop, nothing would have looked suspicious. I was strategizing how witnesses at the strip club would factor into this, anticipating, then boom, he's passing out and I'm skipping it and heading to my place.

I got drive-thru. Him snoring in the passenger seat.

A day later, he was dead. And suicide disappeared as an option.

To be honest, until Schobie's thought showed up, by the time we were out at the lake I was thinking that, hammer aside, this was the world's most underwhelmingly perfect crime. Though, in hindsight, maybe that's a good way for someone who abused fear to die. Underwhelmingly.

And the maker of the wood chipper should be commended, it was weighted so one person can maneuver it around a non-concrete surface like rocks on shore quite well. There was a bigger one in that yard, but I wasn't confident in it being a one-person kind of wood chipper.

Make the body pieces smaller, I told myself. Problem solved.

And the suicide plan vanished because it was replaced with a new post-murder venture. I thought of the economy. Wall Street is too busy auto-fellating to save it. The CEOs can't. But I knew the root cause lay in leadership. I even had a few prospects. Egan wasn't alone in leading this country down.

I also remember thinking, how is a company so fucked up that they create a new management position, in another city no less, pay to relocate and deal with selling his house in this horrible market, all that, just to get him out of Corporate and away from the problems he caused?

Sections of his rib cage, the wood chipper's blades.

They're getting on us more and more about the slightest little expense, then there is Egan. That one harassment case alone.

Some of him, I looked away, grabbed with both hands real quick and threw in the direction of the hopper.

Incompetence. I thought, how many trillions of dollars vanished in the Great Recession due to the pure incompetence of guys like Egan? I said, "Egan, if you were a hard-ass douchebag but a performer and a real leader, we wouldn't be here now."

Forearm, hand, other hand.

That wood chipper was handling it like a champ, though, I had an extra gas jug in the truck if needed. Weight the dropcloth, throw it in, very last thing.

Though the wood chipper needed rethinking as a Disposal Solution. But this wasn't a time-sensitive issue like the Egan disposal issue, so I mentally tabled Ideating for Alternative Disposal Process for later.

I fashioned skiffs for the front wheels of the wood chipper, for pushing along the bottom of the lake. They weren't the most durable, but as long as they held for those fifteen feet, the slight downward slope, the soft but shallow mud. Just like powder, I was thinking. I figured shove with everything I had, no stops, it should gain momentum. The rain and snow were about to hit.

That tack hammer, Doc recommending the thirteen-ounce Light Duty. Out there, I knew the hammer wasn't right. The economy needed something more.

Then, the solution to the hammer question appeared. The missing link to this underwhelmingly perfect crime.

Its strengths as a weapon, our times, its name, their synergy—this couldn't be coincidence. The suicide option was gone for good.

The new plan now even had a uniting theme along with the name.

14

"And folks, The Fear Index has hurtled off to some other Universe and our men and women in uniform are now officially fighting and dying in two wars," Fear says, dressed in a pinstriped suit and flashing neon tie.

Fear and UncertainTina are seated at the news desk, side by side, looking into the camera at you. The blue graphics screen is between them.

UncertainTina's conservative blue business suit is offset by her crimped and teased blonde hair and the lines in her face. Her bangs extend four inches upward, side curls are pronounced, an homage to the year 1987.

The blue screen flashes a graphic:

AXEMAN STRIKES/PRODUCTIVITY UP

UncertainTina says into the camera, "The Axeman claimed his 3627th victim, this time a small-minded Jew-hater who used fear to, as he put it, 'keep his people in line...' He also didn't see the Internet playing a role in the business world and now wanted to eliminate 210 positions. And in other news, managerial inefficiency issues are down, and the economy is picking up steam despite every attempt to fearmonger the world into stagnation. Fear, scientists can't figure this out."

15

"Hammer," I remember yelling, "You...should see the stack...of resumes...on my desk from very well-qualified...axes—"

What Schobie said, roughly 85 percent of Egan had gone through the wood chipper. Thoughts of suicide long gone.

Then, God, that lunch, her voice.

Schobie ran into him with his little boy and wife in a home-improvement store the previous weekend. Bush, yeah, Bush was in office.

"Carrying his boy, he almost looked Dad-like for, what, like, a nanosecond. Definitely wasn't holding a girl. His wife looked like a victim. He looked freaked, like I'd say something— "

I forgot this whole conversation by the time we went back to work. The rest of that day could have been one of five hundred different, unpleasant, unmemorable days.

Then I remembered that conversation. Out there by the lake. Becoming The Axeman was no longer an option. Suicide was no longer an option.

I caught a fish at camp when I was eight. It died in the trash can because I was too afraid to slice it into it.

A few hours after that lunch memory reappeared, as morning neared, I quit huddling in a ball and went to the truck for the extra gas tank.

Then I fed the other 15 percent of Egan into that wood chipper because I made a judgment call at that moment and that made the most sense and in hindsight I don't know, God. Looking at what I had started it just seemed the ultimate disrespect to have what was left out for anybody else to see, I thought I couldn't do that to him, blood was already drying, so I fed him into the wood chipper. It seemed like the professional thing to do. Shoving that thing to the drop-off wasn't as hard as I thought it would be. Just a "1-2-3-GO" and I shoved like nothing else mattered. It's a little over six feet under.

If it's another girl, I'll sell her to an A-rab or some Chink. Carrying his boy, he almost looked Dad-like for a nanosecond.

Turning Your back on someone like me, You were probably thinking, that guy gave up all that? Over fear?

The success of Egan® Disciplinary Fish Food™ so I can employ some people and make sure we get Egan's kids some college educations—we'll shoot for a grad school fund as well—these are the best I can hope for now.

Hey look. Regret.

All of the thoughts about fear and the other emotions, these are good. They'll roll back into the subconscious and intermingle then pop out again later to help solve a future Egan® problem.

Fear, Egan®, the business plan. If it ever feels wrong leveraging fear to steal market share from all those other fish food companies, I'll remind myself that I'm doing this for the employees and Egan's kids' college educations. That third kid, she may end up studying astrophysics and building a rocket ship that can break the speed of light, for all we know.

God, those times here in the office, me going on about how Egan® was going to be the ticket to buying back Egan's soul, well, here and there I might have sounded maybe like I was talking about buying back more than one soul.

I must have sounded pathetic and unprofessional, God, I know. But I couldn't help it. And Egan can't understand what this is like. Not one bit.

When I anonymously set up each of his kids' college funds, I'm going to write each a letter to be sent when they graduate high school, talking about what a great guy he was to work with.

I'm happy to. And I won't be lying.

God, is it okay if I still communicate with Egan, even though he's up there? All this time, with the launch, I kind of need him, if anything to bounce ideas off of.

No, You are right. I'll drop the "kind of."

I don't have anything else besides Egan and Egan®.

I don't even have suicide. The one thing I had, You took from me. And I don't fault You one bit.

Those stories of people who commit acts of rage and then take their own lives afterward, why did You give me a glimpse of where I'd be going?

No. I take that back. That was very smart, killing my weak option before I get to use it.

Look at the first three headlines of this newsfeed.

FEAR PARALYZING WORLD'S STOCK MARKETS

FEAR SLOWING PACE OF NEGOTIATIONS

STUDIES SHOW FEAR INCREASINGLY UNHEALTHY

Do you know what just occurred to me, God, thinking of those company-wide downsizings in '03, '05, and '08, as well as the smaller staffing reductions?

Contrary to what we all say, no one "survives a layoff." Know what happens? They "don't get laid off."

Fear injects death into a situation where it doesn't belong.

Maybe we humans don't have issues with the truth. Just the level of drama in the truth. Like, we deep-down want it to be more exciting than it is, but if we let truth off its leash, that would scare the shit out of us.

So we want life to be boring, but not boring. Fear has a field day with that type of thinking, that confusion. All of the emotions do.

I know you're eternally done with me and aren't hearing a word of this, and I was going to call you every name I could and say everything that one never would think of much less say, but I still can't.

I know where I'm going, but I still can't do that.

Not because I'm afraid of You, but because I love You.

I wish I was worthy enough to fear You again.

GO-TO-MARKET

....

16

Navy One enters the traffic pattern, an invisible, spiraling-downward, racetrack oval that runs counterclockwise in the air around the aircraft carrier *U.S.S. Abraham Lincoln.*

Normally, this flight pattern would be filled with other jets, each descending in its own semi-circular left turn. Each jet forty-five seconds behind the one in front of them, all spiraling downward, centered on the aircraft carrier.

Eventually, each jet reaches that final turn downwind from—to the rear of—the aircraft carrier, for their final approach to land. Right now, Navy One, a four-seat Navy jet called an S-3 Viking, is the only jet in the pattern.

The pilot and co-pilot are in the two front seats. Their passenger is sitting in the back, in the seat where the sonar operator normally sits.

"Hey, since this is a fighter jet, I need a call sign. And where's the turret gun? A squadron of Y2K-Infected Barbarian Sex Cannibals riding Y2K Fire-Breathing Flying Brontosauruses could swoop in."

"Got it covered, Mr. President. For your call sign, how about—"

"How about Donkey-Horse Cock Bowling-Ball Testicles? It conveys that my package is—what's the word—*large.*"

"Doesn't really roll off the tongue, sir—"

The control tower on the *Lincoln* radios in. You and the pilot need to jot down a few quick notes, last-minute details on wind, deck conditions, etc. Standard routine.

The President takes a break from his controls, looks up at you two in the front seat working at your own set of controls. He looks back at his set of controls. Back at your set of controls. Back at his set of controls.

"Wait a minute...I haven't hit any of my buttons...but we are still flying...Don't make...me...get...elliptical...here..."

You and your pilot look at each other.

Navy One passes up the starboard side of the ship, tailhook down, descending. Final pass upwind. At a point past the bow of the ship—out in front of it a quarter of a mile, the pilot will make a hard left turn called the break turn, throttle back to idle, extend the speed brakes. Then, he'll extend and lock the landing gear as the plane U-turns back and makes its final pass down the port side of the ship.

The break turn's purpose is to kill your speed by turning your airframe perpendicular, into the incoming jetstream. Turn the plane's physical surface sideways, so instead of shooting on a knife-edge into that jetstream, your wide surfaces are at right angles to it. Counteracting all of the laws of physics you were obeying to stay in the air.

Kill airspeed quickly, glide in to the deck.

After the break turn, Navy One will make one final pass down the port side to a point past the stern of the carrier, before that final ninety-degree turn downwind. When the jet rolls out of this final turn, the deck will be straight ahead out of the cockpit windshield.

Eventually, the theory goes, the tailhook protruding from underneath the plane will grab one of four arresting cables at the stern of the ship.

It's a delicate act, never the same flight twice. Directional conditions, aircraft weight, time of day, windspeeds—all of these vary. Fly long enough, this becomes a personal competition: how to line your aircraft up more precisely each time, letting gravity and airspeed slow your descent. You're not flying anymore, you're gliding. Those properties you depend on to stay aloft, you reject in order to land—

"Hey! Watch this—"

He grabs the plastic steering wheel taped to the control panel in front of him and cranks it back and forth about twenty times.

Navy One continues its slow left-veering course, not even a small jolt.

"I knew it! You…"

You and your pilot look at each other.

Passing up the starboard side of the carrier.

"For the sake of National Job Suck-Curity, I…," his eyes narrow, "order…you…those…controller…plane-flying…things dotdotdot—"

Your pilot is at a loss, too.

Navy One passes the bow of the carrier. Break turn, less than twenty seconds away.

What does one do? Disobey a direct order from The Commander In Chief of The United States of America? That sounds like a court martial-worthy offense.

No. Better idea.

You turn to your President, hook your thumbs underneath your armpits and scream,

"FLAP, MR. PRESIDENT, FLAP!"

as you start to flap your arms.

Your President flaps his arms, tentatively at first, outstretched, not hooking his thumbs underneath his armpits. His arms, especially the right one, which is right by the window, repeatedly bang against controls and the sides of the aircraft.

"Like this?" your President asks.

"No, sir, hook your thumbs, like this!" The President hooks his thumbs and flaps furiously.

Five seconds until the break turn.

"HARDER, SIR! FLAP HARDER! BOUNCE UP AND DOWN IN YOUR SEAT. YOU HAVE A PLANE TO LAND, MR. PRESIDENT."

Break turn. The pilot rolls the plane hard left. When the aircraft slows like this, it creates negative gravity. You feel the weightlessness and static floods your earphones. That's the wind's response to you all messing with the laws of flight.

The pilot descends the landing gear as Navy One begins its final downwind leg, traveling down the port side of the carrier. Your President's breathing through his oxygen mask fills the earpieces in your headset.

After about ten seconds of flapping, he stops and points.

"Look! Your face! Y2K Innards-Falling-Out Syn—"

"THAT'S MY OXYGEN MASK. FLAP, MR. PRESID—DONKEY-HORSE COCK BOWLING-BALL TESTICLES—FLAP! WE ARE DRIFTING BELOW GLIDE SLOPE. FLAP."

He is back to flying, flapping away. Navy One's rate of descent increases. Not even a minute from the arresting cables on the carrier deck, one of which your tailhook will grab. In theory.

Your pilot rolls out of the final bank and evens the wings out. The deck of the carrier is straight ahead and getting closer.

"Flying airplanes…it's hard work."

"WE GOT A PLANE TO LAND, DONKEY-HORSE COCK BOWLING-BALL TESTICLES!"

His visor is filled with fog. Flapping. Flapp—

Navy One's tailhook snares the three wire. Full stop in under two seconds.

Mission accomplished.

17

Little Miss Doubt finishes fluffing her red hair and applying her lipstick right before the camera rolls.

"Unfortunately, last night my brother Fear started off with an Arkansas River of vodka and finished with a Hoover Dam of pharmaceuticals and a Long Island of Long Island Iced Teas so I'll be filling in as your anchor for today. Don't miss Doctor Igno's upcoming interview with the best-selling author of *The Shit-Fucking Dance: A Manager's Guide To 21st-Century Workplace Productivity*.

And on our sister channel, the silly one for younger kids, we're going to throw Fear's apprehensive man-assistant Sivvie into a vat of gasoline and light it on fire.

That new practical joke show is taking off.

And now, as I deliver the data regarding American corporations shipping jobs overseas over the course of the first decade, would you like me to soften the negativity of this news by sucking on this grape lollipop or the cherry one? Text *3452 for grape and *3454 for cherry."

18

How is it that I am in business with a guy who not only voted for that guy twice, but also had a little "W" sticker on his SUV?

Times change, Egan. Times change.

Getting back from the fish food conference, no one is thinking the disciplinary angle. We're inventing a new curve here, we're that far ahead. I had to cup my hand over my mouth the whole time.

I wanted to meander through that crowd of cutting-edge fish food executives, sidle up, look one in the eye and whisper, "Is your current fish doing the job dotdotdot" or "keep them 85 percent satisfied" or "keep those fish on their 'toes,'" then sidle away. But we're not far enough along yet.

Also, I went by Harvard since I was in town. I can totally see at least one of your kids going to Harvard.

One thing I did notice, though, most of those conference people talked endlessly about being in fear for their jobs. Glad you and I aren't shackled to that life any more, am I right?

Homie, I feel like you and I, after that decade, we are the only two beings who aren't addicted to fear. All the other emotions, too.

Not judging, I was once where all those other people are now, back in cubicle/pre-murder life. But still. We have yet to turn a profit, still being in the incubation stage, and we're spending the Egan® capital, but I just feel so much positivity.

It's weird, believing in yourself these days. And maybe there's the double aspect of using fear to sell Egan®, coupled with so much fear in the air.

And this all started with me living in fear. You know, I saw a figure on that decade, and it said that antidepressant use from 2005-2010 rose by 40 percent or more, I think it was a European study.

Later discussion: anti-depressants in fish food: yes or no. Sampling meeting.

But tell me that the IDK decade brand of fear we're talking about, in terms of leveraging for Egan®, is just a mirage. Tell me that decade didn't change us as people.

I just got a message from a friend of mine.

She's a New Yorker. Long Islander, now in Manhattan. If she found a cockroach in her apartment, she'd catch it and take it outside.

One morning, she shot seven rolls of film. Film. Yeah, that stuff. She's an artist, only allows a few people to see these photographs. My friend lives in the West Village in New York City.

She shot these rolls of film from her rooftop on the morning of September 11, 2001.

Thirty or forty blocks from, well, you know.

This just in: dozens of people are reported dead.

Maybe three and a half years later, I received an e-mail from her. It was a group e-mail, very long, addressed to lots of people. She and her boyfriend wrote the e-mail from a public computer terminal at the airport in Colombo, Sri Lanka. They were wearing the same pairs of shorts, sandals, and t-shirts for the past three days.

Three days earlier was the first morning since their arrival that they skipped surfing first thing in the morning. On this day, they decided to drive down the coast for lunch at a lobster shack instead.

They were on vacation with her boyfriend's family, his sisters, and their families. In the water in front of their beach house was a coral reef. The boyfriend wrote in the e-mail that this sea wall bought members of his family some added escape time.

This just in: reports are flowing in the death toll is rising.

On their drive down the coast, my friend and her boyfriend stopped to check out an old fort. This delayed them from driving through a crowded coastal town that suffered massive casualties when the first waves hit. They were on the bridge entering the town when their driver first pointed out the roads on the other side.

It looked like a water main broke.

Their driver was turning their vehicle around on that bridge when they looked back at the buses and trucks and cars crashing down the streets and into buildings as that water rose, reaching rooftop levels.

Racing off that bridge on the other side, their driver took them through yards and gardens, behind houses, bursting through fences, until they found an opening to a road that took them inland to higher elevation.

Both survivors from the coast and people who lived farther inland crowded that road. The first group wanted safety. The second, information.

This just in: the death toll could potentially run into the hundreds.

My friend. 9/11. The Tsunami.

I knew her years before that, in the '90s. Gentle, smart. Long Island girl's worldliness. She never aimed or schemed to get men to buy her drinks—this just in: estimates of the dead are now definitely in the hundreds—men just bought her drinks.

My feeling is that these men saw a woman way out of their league, and went for it. But most importantly, they woke up the next day feeling proud that they weren't chicken-shit.

She is hot as anything, yet human. They didn't hook up, but these men tried. For this, these guys were proud of themselves.

That old saying: you strike out 100 percent—

This just in: Indonesia, Thailand, and India were struck too. The death toll is in the thousands—

You strike out 100 percent of the times you don't step up to the plate.

Cool thing about her was that she wasn't the slightest bit derogatory about any of these men. She was genuinely open to the idea that one of them could be cool. She's also confident enough with who she is to set her standards where she set them.

She looked down on women who made it a point to scam drinks, then brag about playing the situation the entire time. This just in: scientists estimate that the Tsunami unleashed a force over 1502 times the size of The Atomic Bomb.

This also just in: death estimates reach the tens of thousands.

Oh yeah—this is just in: indigenous cultures are gone forever.

Passing the halfway point of the first decade of the third millennium, I just felt used to all of the negativity in the world. Looking back, being in fear for my job, whatever, it just occurred to me that I was pretty ho-hum reading her e-mail for a good while. Fear makes you numb.

And know what's weird? I can remember thinking the Tsunami is a much needed, if temporary, diversion from everything else. Iraq, this was when they were finding piles of bodies in villages I think, like on a daily basis. Civilians.

And for work, the walking on eggshells with layoffs, the negativity is what got me through it all.

Oh yeah, get this pisser of a wrench in the wheel: a couple of years after The Tsunami, my friend got prescribed a medication that put her in a coma for a while, then all that health insurance crap on top of everything.

Fear, like when it shows up, it wants to hear your every thought about this world. About this crazy little thing called life. Look at every website featuring pictures of bodies blown apart. By the middle of this first decade, negativity was a power source.

Fear loves it when I wonder why she had to have front row seats to not one but both of these events, then suffered a medical emergency on top. This just in: the death toll is at least in the hundreds of thousands. Expected to still climb.

This just in: We haven't even mentioned Hurricane Katrina, The Florida Hurricanes, the Pakistan, Iran, China, and India earthquakes. The Haiti Earthquake happened twelve days into the next decade, but we'll mention it here, too. All that force released in a span of ten years. Take a second and imagine all of that force, combined.

This just in: all of that force would disintegrate you like you were hurtling through the center of the Sun.

My friend left me a message a week ago. And with all that—oh I didn't bring her up in the present. She's alive today. Recovering from all three events. Living. Doing her thang. As far as I know, beginning the second decade, just like the rest of us. Just trying to figure all of this out. And she's much more positive than many people I know.

Like me.

I can't ever speak to her again.

I'm never going to meet your kids. I don't even know their names. Don't want to. We'll have to figure that out when the bank accounts need to get set up.

If I'm not in the office tomorrow or the next day researching those disciplinary fish food trends for that sales preso, blame the Universe.

It will be reminding me that murdering you was the worst idea I ever had.

19

I bet some European company will get in the game.

Deesceepleenaree feesh fud.

Sorry. That's Egan's "Get-To-Work" look. I had another vision, homeslice. No.

This is it: we need to think bigger and realize what we, being disciplinary fish food titans, what we need to accomplish here. Your kids' college educations, obviously, 'nuff said. But quit thinking about that supply chain problem for a second and picture how we need to think about who we're employing. This is how you fit into the Egan® business model, your role going forward, even though you're actually in Heaven.

We're at the Egan® Disciplinary Fish Food Factory—or, is it Plant?

Whatever, it's Monday morning. The line of workers is waiting to punch in. Readying themselves to take their place on the assembly line. The Day Shift relieving the Graveyard Shift. As it's been done so many times over the years, all across America. In countless industries.

Keeping the assembly line going is an American ritual.

Those new Egan® workers, as they're punching in, will be wondering if Egan is some kind of superhero, that's why you never see him but always feel the Egan presence, the older workers will say, yes.

In a way, Egan *is* a superhero, yes. As they're clocking in, all of those workers will say, Thank you, Egan. Thank you for everything. The job. The opportunity. Each and every worker will want to retire from Egan®.

Only that retirement day seems long off to these workers, in that good kind of way.

At Egan®, employees are excited to retire, but they can wait to retire. They have a good, steady job. Family-friendly benefits, profit sharing, flat, top-light not-heavy management structure, they believe in Egan®. They believe in their livelihoods.

Imagine that: a world where people believe in their livelihoods again—DUDE—

Egan® Disciplinary Fish Food needs a mascot.

HOW LONG HAVE WE BEEN IN BUSINESS AND NOT HAD A MASCOT?

Like the Egan® Y2K Fire-Breathing Flying Brontosaur—No, good call, not family-friendly. Egan® the Dog? Like a watch dog—Egan® the Disciplinary Alien—

Egan®, the, the, the—eagle?

Egan the Eagle®!

DUUUUUUUUUDE—start looking at illustrator's portfolios immediately! Once, you were human. Then you were fish food. Next, you became a brand. Now, Egan® is a mascot—

With any luck, one day Egan® will be an icon. Get some, homie. Git SOME. Wait. Waitwaitwait, are you seeing it too? Out in front of the factory?

A 12-foot-high Egan® the Eagle mascot statue, either bronze or in the company's colors. Egan®. Standing tall or whatever it is that eagles do. Wait—

Are we liking the whole Egan® the Eagle concept just because it rolls off the tongue? Is the eagle the right mascot? Bake on this. May wake up and hate it. What?

What?

Dude, this vibe is good. Why do you have to point to that bill tacked up on the wall?

Yeah, I knew it was there. And still unpaid. Believe me, I know. We're a startup. Money dwindles when startups start up.

Enough of that negativity, look at this business. It's like everything that crashed our economy, we're packaging it up and putting your kids through college.

Is your current fish food doing the job dotdotdot.

And I gotta say it: squatting at your place of residence which now happens to be your business sounds like how Egan® rolls. These times we're in, this is the company that tells The Great Recession to go suck a syphilitic dick, am I right or am I right?

This is a way to look at Egan®.

The top bottled water brand pulled in about four billion dollars last year.

But go back in time thirty to forty years. Ask mankind if they would pay big bucks—no, any money period—for water. For water, they would look at you, "really?" Tell them that in the future people will participate in consumer promotions, for water.

Hey, buy water, enter to win a trip to all the waterparks in the U.S. Staring at aisles of brands of water in various shaped bottles, some crystal clear, others colored, mythic waterfall here, Arctic glacier there, idealized water molecule over there.

They would look at you and say, "but…it's water…"

And they wouldn't be using the ellipses like some insecure manager, either. They'd be confused as all get out. Water…They'd…Be… Saying…

Who says that Disciplinary won't be like that in twenty years? We just have to figure out how to capitalize on all the fear in the air.

Another product to look at: vodka. Used to be vodka, yes, I know it's early, fuck off, I'm hungover, vodka was what alcoholics drank because the booze didn't show up on their breath.

No one paid fifteen hundred dollars to have one bottle of vodka brought to their poolside table. Vodka? Who gives a shit what country the hobos' drink comes from? Vodka—

Dude, not like I have any meetings today it's cool—

But that's how we have to think. With Egan® and the whole Disciplinary thing.

It's like that decade, trying not to waste more energy labeling the rights versus wrongs but just see things for what they are.

Egan® is making progress. One of us, hinthinthint, needs to get on the Figuring Out How To Make Fish Food project.

We also need to get some legal documents drawn up. A company this size needs legal documents. Once we have a logo, we'll affix said logo to these documents. Egan® The Eagle would make a cool logo.

Man, lawyers are expensive. Any ideas? Wait...

I'm not dotdotdotting like a layer of management here, I have an idea.

20

"Doc, thanks for signing on as Egan®'s legal counsel, free of charge, no less."

"No problem. Fear Indexes Hold 'Em last month, I cleared two grand. Besides, I don't have a law degree and am preemptively disbarred in the first place, so free seems right."

"Great price for a startup, too."

"Son, I admire you disciplinary fish food pros, charging forward in this climate of fear. Those other execs cowering in their corners, you guys—can he hear me?"

"Yes, Doc. Egan says he can hear you fine."

"But you said he can't talk."

"Yeah, right, I *said*. Doc, you don't understand, starting a business with somebody, you get to know each other's mannerisms."

"I went through a Send-Those-Apparitions-Back-To-Where-They-Came-From phase, but I got over that negativity."

"Doc, sorry, but Egan and I have—"

"Yesyes. Legal. My advice, gentlemen: Legalese is all about fear. Egan® is a company that capitalizes on fear, yet operates without fear. So as a company Egan® needs to achieve that Universally-aligned state of being known as Legaleselessness."

"Legaleselessness?"

"Yes. Who wants to talk legalese when there are other subjects, like mermaids? Instead of composing a bunch of legalese for you, I thought, the world has enough legalese. What it lacks is pictures of mermaids painted by a person who just ingested five uppers and two trucks of wine. I did this four-by-six-foot painting for your office, isn't that nice?"

"Well, Doc, *my* first thought on seeing that mermaid—while I do agree that Legaleselessness sounds like a fantastic state of company being for Egan®—first thought was that mermaids were the hallucinations of pirates. Some of said pirates died out at sea without ever physically holding another woman and pirates are often used as a metaphor for ex-big-ship ex-Corporate entrepreneurial types. But the SECOND thought, based on the first thought, is that murder negates the idea of me loving again, so I'll probably be out of the office for the next three days outside screaming at the Sun begging for forgiveness hope the cops don't show again last time wasn't good. Besides that, I'm liking. Egan? Of course he likes it.

Gotta switch gears here. Doc, I also wanted to bring you in because I hate to put my partner on the spot, but I thought having our Legal Counsel in this talk could be good. Egan, my friend: with all of the Egan® projects I have going, you taking the making of the fish food off of my plate would be a big help—"

"Son, I can't see the guy, but I'm sure Egan is giving you the ol' I-wanna-meet-your-parents-and-facepunch-them look right now. Think of how Egan joined this enterprise. Dead or alive, people are people."

"Wow, Doc. I never thought—Egan, I'm sorry—"

"No point in beating yourself up, if anyone would understand this situation and the lack of human understanding here, it would be Egan. And you, you should think of this as a lesson, for when you start employing people. I have an idea: since I still have about six brain cells left that are familiar with biology and chemistry, I'll figure out this fish food. Taking a break from 'Dex slingin' will be nice."

"Doc, really?"

"No problem. Good leaders delegate to experts. First thought, fish food: microscopic handcuffs—"

"Doc, that would be amazing. With you as our Senior Counsel/Chief Fish Food Engineering Officer—"

"Glad I'm here. Leaders bring in experts in fields to help them reach their vision. And you two: seeking to revolutionize the fish food industry without in fact knowing how to make fish food...I'm not acting like a manager here, I'm just thinking…About the beauty…Compared to the business world in 2010 this company is doing just fine. You. Umm, could you step outside with me, away from Egan, walk with me—"

"Hey Egan, is it cool if us fleshyfolk talk, cool? Good. I'll just be a sec. Okay, Doc, what's up?"

"Egan may have been the inspiration for Egan®, but he was also a human being once and you ended his life. Job Creator, you may be trailblazing new trails in business, but we all *are* or *were* human beings here. A true leader never loses sight of that. These days these leaders think they can squeezesqueezesqueeze and greed their people to death. You don't want to be one of them, do you?"

"Of course not, Doc. I'd shoot myself first. And I know where I'm going when I die."

"If you want to lead a company of thousands possibly trillions of fish food professionals you'd best look at your people skills. Since you possess a soul that's forever destroyed and worthless, you see money for what it is, right?"

"Doc, I'd trade all of the Egan® assets and Go-To-Market thinking for a chance to hang out with my soul in its old form for an hour again and say that living in fear isn't worth it."

"Perfect. Look at the poeticism: a soulless CEO teaching the world what it's like to run a company of human beings in the second decade of this new millennium. Son, our world is stagnant when it needs to be vibrant. All of that fear is freezing us in place, leadership at all levels has become dependent on it. Fear is killing innovation, that beautiful lifeblood. You hated the house of cards called Corporate America to the point where you committed the unpardonable. Now that business world needs a new business paradigm that doesn't thrive on fear and hanging on to that inefficiency-based status quo."

"And I always thought trailblazing a new industry would be so easy."

"Son, think about this: it's fifty years from now. We're gone, Egan® has been sold and is now twenty times as big. The R&D budget alone runs into the tens of millions. Only the Egan® offices and drive-thru stations in every country are in chaos, problems we can't fathom. Add this wrench to the wheel: Egan® is also part of a larger entity which adds new dimensions to the issues. They need somebody who operates on that macro level, combining markets and negotiating treaties—and keeping shareholders happy. The Board interviews hundreds of candidates. She's Law School, MBA, Green Beret. Been a COO here, CFO there, now it's her turn at President. She's got a couple of rugrats at home, good husband. Now, Egan® is bursting with problems to solve, and she ain't afraid. This incoming President, who withstood the rigorous interview process of that Corporation's board, do you know what her maiden name could possibly be?"

"I don't know, Doc."

"That's a decade, son, not a name. Think. Be optimistic. There is a universe of possibilities out there."

"Egan?"

"Yup. That third daughter. Her maiden name, no one knows, not even her. The press release people will probably use it for human interest/ain't-that-a-coincidence spin before she goes and makes that big speech to the shareholders."

"I can hear her speech now. And since I can't find any management book that doesn't talk about using fear, I'm going to have to make this up as I go along. That idea doesn't scare me one bit."

"Now you're wrapping your head around it. Think of all those future Egan® managers you will train that will learn the Egan® way and take their fear-free business know-how to other companies. Business write-ups will turn into management books about the next wave in business. The Egan® way."

"Egan econ—Egan®omics, I see it, Doc."

"Peel away that veil of fear and look around, son. Our world doesn't need another revolution. All it needs is some revolutionizing."

21

The camera cuts to Fear, who is leaning back in his studio chair. The microphone attached to Fear's collar is a bit off-kilter, the bangs are falling out of place down onto Fear's forehead. Fear is chuckling as if talking to somebody off camera.

"He didn't—HE DID NOT JUST SAY 'YOU GO TO WAR WITH THE ARMY YOU HAVE NOT THE ARMY YOU MIGHT WANT OR WISH TO HAVE AT A LATER TIME'—during Ratings Week—to answer one of our own troop's honest and straightforward questions, in front of our own troops, WITH THE CAMERA ROLLING—"

22

"Our first, most obvious target audience is people who own fish, right?

The genius of where the Egan® brand is headed is that this target audience is age, gender, political affiliation, and demo-psycho-graphic neutral.

They own fish. Fish that need to be kept in line. But we're not thinking big enough yet. Think of all of those people who hesitate to buy fish—who really want to own fish, but don't think they can.

Their barrier to entry—to becoming fish owners—Egan® is the solution.

This disciplinary niche market may not be a niche after all. Think about what the initial target market, fish owners, knows that the next group of potential customers doesn't know. If we figure out how to communicate what they know to those who don't know, there's opportunity here.

Our Phase Two Expansion Market.

They see the Early Adapters, current fish owners, purchasing Egan® by the fishtankfull and—

While we're gaining extra brand loyalty with the current fish owners, we create brand loyalty with a whole new, ever-expanding group— that's always desired to be fish owners!

Egan® doesn't just make money off the current customer base. It creates new customer bases. It's the gateway brand for non-fish owners. Their barrier of entry is the disciplinary issue. Egan® would be the answer. After Phase Two, we do this right, we got Phases Three through—

And we're still not thinking big enough yet—

Think of all of the ancillary industries that Egan® will reinvigorate.

The Fish Tank, Fish Tank Lightbulb, the Fish Tank Water Pump Industries. The Neon Rock Industry. The Miniature Ceramic Pirate Ship Industry.

The Plastic Sea Plant Industry. Think about all those out-of-work plastic sea plant farmers Egan® is going to save.

And right now some person is sitting in a cubicle, dreaming of constructing a miniature ceramic pirate ship, then sailing it out to sea, sinking it, raising it from the bottom, then selling it to somebody, so they can put it in their fish tank.

They're living in fear at that miserable job and putting that dream in a drawer. And then they start to notice the increasing number of fish tanks. So they're brushing up on their ceramics and sailing lessons. But they're hesitating. But if Disciplinary creates enough new fish tank owners, sooner or later these people will be flying the ceramic pirate flag. That's how we need to approach this.

Pure capitalism, only symbiotic and mutually beneficial. It's time to revolutionize. Capitalism 2.0. Egan® could—

Could God-friggin-damn well revive our flagging economy. That's what it could do. Look in the news, all the other corporations and their CEOs are cowering in fear here in this second decade.

The concept of capitalism has been perverted and twisted into something that it so isn't, maybe Egan® will be the first step toward bringing this back. Yoooooo-yo-yo-yoooooooo—the Oxygen-Pump-Disguised-As-Plastic-Miniature-Deep-Sea-Diving-Man Industry—Egan® could revolutionize that too.

And still, we're not thinking big enough yet.

Here's an example of the untapped potential, using a subset of our target market: hippies.

We got two types of hippies here. Type One Hippie doesn't own a TV and instead pulls tubes and watches their fish swim around while listening to nineteen-minute songs.

Type Two Hippie smokes their weed while watching TV. Reruns mainly. No fish. Or nineteen-minute songs.

They deep down would rather be pulling tubes and watching live fish, while listening to long—we're talking very long—songs. But there, again, is that whole barrier-to-entry thing.

Egan® is their gateway to owning their own fish tank. Disciplinary issue covered, that tank is bought. IF we do this launch right.

And let's think bigger: all of these hippies order late night delivery. I'm just extrapolating here: but the non-fish owners would order more late-night food if they gazed at their fish tanks versus their television sets. As opposed to TV, the human imagination and honkingly-long songs stimulate the appetite, energizing the mind and neurons.

I acknowledge that this is a complete hunch.

But work with me here: TV and computers spoon-feed everything and keep the mind passive. And that's a rerun they're watching anyway.

On the other hand, a fish tank full of the correct mix of fish is random, unpredictable. Technology is passive, a fish tank is alive.

This makes the mind hungry. Works up the mental appetite. Plus, if you're stoned, grooving to a jam while looking at your fish—

Instead of watching that rerun where that guy—see you know it already—our Phase Two market is staring at the fish in their brand-new fish tank complete with new water pump and organically-grown plastic sea plants and knowing that Egan® is there just in case and these hippies are letting their mind race.

They're watching the fish. At that point in the song where most people would be thinking 'Is this song stuck?' they'll be thinking 'If a fish got elected President, and went on a diplomatic mission to another country, and the ceremonial dinner was fish sticks, that would probably cause some type of war.'

The key here: minds are racing again.

That's what the world needs: more minds need to rediscover the lost art of racing.

Egan® could resurrect America. Egan® could—What if somebody starts a late-night delivery business, HotWingzN'PuffyChipsN'Frozen-YogurtN'DietSoda™?

But, they would have never started it if it weren't for Egan®. Egan® expands their pool of potential customers. No: it inspires entrepreneurialism. If Egan® didn't exist, HotWingzN'PuffyChipsN'FrozenYogurt-N'DietSoda® could never exist.

Yeah, that's right: registration mark is no longer pending. Are you getting in on the HotWingzN'PuffyChipsN'FrozenYogurtN'DietSoda® IPO? I sure am.

But these budding entrepreneurs, today they don't believe the potential customer base is there. Egan® will help create it for them.

They would do a 'before/after study' around the launch of Egan®, watching Pizza Tent® and WokFalafelTacoSausage® and their late-night delivery numbers after the giant infusion of all that disciplinary fish food into the marketplace.

They'll see this market's potential. And think: this is just a tiny portion of the Egan® target market.

And also: in terms of consumers, remember these people will also be bailing out the Plastic-Miniature-Deep-Sea-Diver-Whoa-Holyshit-It's-Really-An-Undercover-Water-Pump Industry.

Egan® is capitalism at its best.

This is, this is—I'm trailing off here, guys, sorry—just started thinking about those checks I just wrote and all that money, that threw off my mojo. I've been working day and night, too. Sorry guys. Doc, what do you think?"

"Well, son, I don't know what Egan® here thinks, but I think it should get investors interested. Every other industry is hopped up on panic and those self-absorbed money autojerkoffs got their pants around their ankles, the world needs disciplinary fish fooders like you to light the way. If that danged Egan weren't on another vacation we could get his two cents."

"Cut Egan some slack for not being around the office, Doc, he might not be with us much longer. But that portrait of Egan riding off into the sunset on that cockamamie dickheadbike he used to ride into work on Fridays will always hang proudly in our future lobby. Egan®, what did you think of my 'elevator speech?'"

"I don't know, the opening should be quicker. What do you think, Doc?"

"Quicker, good call, Egan®. Listen to this nine-foot-tall, pastel-colored bird, son. And Egan®: how fortunate is this company that your professional background doesn't just lie in the mascot industry, but also includes two previous stints as CFO?"

23

The First Decade of The Third Millennium draws to a close. He is behind his desk. Corner office, fifty stories up. He is the master, of this space. The master. This space.

He loosens his belt, unzips his fly, pulls up his computer's slideshow program. He has over nine hundred pictures on disk from his recent vacation. Aruba.

Every picture has one commonality: him. A Wall Street Master of The Universe.

Who is about to masturbate to over nine hundred new pictures of himself.

Bow-ch-ch-chi-BOW

Bow-ch-ch-chi-BOW

If people worked less and masturbated to pictures of themselves more, this world would be—

Wait. Why think about *that* when you can think about yourself? And your Self.

This is Wall Street. Masturbationally masterful.

Fuck the financial carpet being pulled out from under you.

The government will bail you out. Bow-ch-ch-chi-BOW.

The pictures are loading. Afternoon calendar is cleared. The underlings will have to survive.

The, how to put it?—deferred, post-dated—however you put that deal together, whatever you embellished, guess what? This is success.

You wanna fuck with Wall Street? Our motto is "You fuck with us, we'll hire a kick-ass consulting firm. Then we'll masturbate to pictures of ourselves."

Aw yeah.

Now-this-is-HOW-you-Bow-ch-ch-chi-BOW.

The slideshow readies.

Looking for Aruba scenery shots? Buy a coffee table book.

Multi-tasking like a God Among Men. Lubing up, finger-limbering exercises, popping a quick mint.

Some people are better than others.

You soooo bow-ch-ch-chi-BOW.

People don't know what it's like to masturbate to pictures of yourself. And your Self.

To those who lost their savings, sorry. But on a more important note: Spank, monkey, spank.

TARP, bailout, TARP.

Bow-ch-ch-chi—you just learned how to talk dirty to yourself—BOW.

You've evolved. Fuck this economy.

You, and every picture of you, are economy-proof.

You slay dragons, navigating funds through the market, finding ways to hide those losses.

This is your boner—bonus, we're talking about.

You reached that astral plane. Guess what we do up here?

Aw yeah.

Time to squeeze out some questionable sales data.

Aruba.

Spartan warriors look down from the Heavens, wishing they could be you, wishing—

YYESSSS—You. Tailored suit and Spartan warrior helmet. Professionally lit and shot in a studio—masturbating to that, possibly even frame a copy for your secretary—that would bow-ch-ch-chi-SO-BOW.

You, there, on the portside deck, in that fishing chair. That Ultra-Heavy, throbbing pole protruding from between your legs.

No tuna can handle this pole.

And there you are, holding up said tuna you caught with your Ultra-Heavy pole. Oh, yes. Yesss. That tuna must be a female dog. BECAUSE IT IS MOST DEFINITELY YOUR BITCH. Yesss.

Fighter pilot style. Yyesssssssss…
Here you go: a Spartan warrior/fighter pilot/tailored suit outfit.
Pose in some studio wearing that. The checking-the-watch pose…
You'd self-hit that to that. Hell yes you would.
You, jet skiing. So much high-octane power between your legs.
Pause. Lube break—
Play—
The waiter agreed to pose for this next shot. Tipping him a single dollar bill after that $1340 tab, him faking that thankful look on his face. You, staring at the camera like the Master of The Universe that you are. And of course he got his ten percent.

You, posing with those bikini babes from—where were they from—you don't touch yourself much to this one—wait—good GOD they frame your physique nicely.

Your fish are swimmin'.

You're thinking Africa next. Oh, the pictorial possibilities. You, with dead animals you paid to kill. Posing with scenery, maybe the land that a company you have interest in is looking to purchase and mine for diamonds. Get a shot of it with you now. Before it is destroyed. Get a before/after shot of yourself with this land.

Masturbating to these two shots, oh that will be the day.

Maybe with some black women. Frame you, in between a couple of them, the skin contrast outlining your body, yesssss.

Plus, you have a set position in the company who produces the lo-tion you're lubing Adonis with right now. Not only are you an owner, you're also a customer.

Back to these pictures. The Aruba pictures.

You, with the view from your hotel balcony, the bay is behind you. If anybody knows how to pose, it's you, stallion.

You, with that whale jumping out of the water, maybe two hundred feet behind your boat. You have a stake in a Japanese company that hunts whales and processes maybe 50 percent of the body, lets the other rot.

Whales WISH they could masturbate to pictures of themselves.

Here. On the restaurant deck in the bay. That pose, appearing so relaxed. Toasting the camera with that umbrella drink. The seventy-ninth umbrella drink of the day.

She was in this picture too. Wait—the wife??? How did this shot—this is the "Yourself" folder, how did she get in here? This is unconscionable—once you and Adonis are through working your magic, it's time to fire that secretary.

Take a deep breath.

Oh well, you were tiring of her anyway.

The secretary. Not the wife.

Haven't had a good firing in a while anyway, rev up the fear, keep the underlings on their toes.

Back to Yourself.

And your Self.

In that tourist shop, trying on funny hats. Why? To show that you don't take yourself seriously. You try on funny hats.

Good God you are funny when you try on funny hats and pose for the camera and don't take yourself seriously. Good God.

Adonis is on the prowl. You create wealth.

You have superpowers. Wielding these, manipulating data.

Spank, monkey, spank.

TARP, bailout, TARP.

Spank, monkey, spank.

TARP, bailout, TARP.

24

Baby Nicky's panicky zombie-toddler bald head and old-person-waiting-to-die yellow veiny eyes fill the screen. Baby Nicky lunges through the screen.

"PATRIOTACTPATRIOTACTPATRIO—"

Change the channel. Remote control, work your magic. Please work your magic.

Fear is now bald, black suit, white shirt, paisley tie. Fear's apprehensive man-assistant Sivvie is still in the frame talking to Fear.

Fear is saying, "Dammit, Sivvie, is Monsieur E's satellite feed out AGAIN? It's Ratings Week—"

Fear sees that the camera is rolling and face-punches Sivvie as hard as Fear can to get Sivvie out of the shot, then Fear straightens its collar and turns back to the camera.

"This just in from Iraq. Can you hear us, UncertainTina?"

The screen cuts to the field, where UncertainTina is wearing a culturally-sensitive headdress, along with that black leather miniskirt that doesn't look nearly as good on her as it once did.

She's standing in front of a makeshift tent in the desert. "Fear, Uday and Qusay Hussein are laid out on two metal tables, side by side. Their bodies, done up like wax museum statues, are lying there." She and the camera crew walk into the tent and show you, the viewers, those bodies.

Fear interrupts and the camera cuts back to Fear in the newsroom.

"So, UncertainTina, so those are stitched-up, y-shaped autopsy scars on each of their torsos, not some new Iraqi necktie trend? They are a different culture, you know."

UncertainTina turns from the bodies and looks into the camera. "Those are incisions, Fear. Yes indeed."

"So...they're dead?"

UncertainTina speaks into the microphone, "Yes, Fear. I even poked each body with a stick to see if they would move, and they didn't. They are indeed dead."

"Thanks Tina. And now viewers, we take you to the US-Mexico border where Doctor Igno and The Less Triplets are standing by. Doctor Igno?"

Doctor Igno is standing by a muddy river wearing khakis and a blue polo shirt holding the microphone. Bald head, wire-framed eyeglasses, he's partially squinting and the wind is blowing as he holds his hand to his ear.

The Less sisters are behind him in the background of the shot, ankle deep in the water. Each is wearing a string bikini and sombrero and undulating slowly for the camera.

Doctor Igno says, "Fear, we were going to report on the tens of thousands of Mexicans that were killed in the first decade of the millennium due to the narco violence. But since this is Ratings Week, we decided to use this location to report on the United States population reaching the three hundred million mark during that decade instead. Back to you."

"Real quickly, folks, back to UncertainTina, who is in Karachi, Pakistan," Fear says. The camera cuts.

UncertainTina is wearing a culturally sensitive Muslim headdress, along with skin-tight leopard skin pantsuit and spiked boots. She's standing by a dirt road, a cloud of smoke is rising in the distance. She turns to the camera.

"A wedding in Pakistan was interrupted—not by the bride's old boyfriend barging in and announcing to everyone that the bride and groom were never meant to be and he is the one. No, it wasn't that. It was an erroneously targeted missile strike."

The news channel cuts back to Fear who sends it to Little Miss Doubt, out in the field. She's wearing a low-cut cowgirl outfit, holding her earphone to her ear with one hand, the microphone with the other, in the middle of this Texas tumbleweed-filled field, staring into the camera.

"Do NOT get in the way of a Vice President and his shotgun."

She points the mike to the camera. "Pow." She then blows the smoke out of the tip of the mike, just like a pistol. She winks. "Back to you, Fear."

The camera cuts back to Fear, now grey-haired, in a blue pin-striped suit, sitting in a high-backed leather chair by a fake fireplace. The camera zooms in for a commentary close-up on Fear:

"When he got the official word through his earpiece that President John F. Kennedy died, Walter Cronkite teared up, choked up on camera, lost his composure, and cried along with the world. He reported to a stunned planet, brought it along minute by minute as this same world-altering event was unfolding in front of him. Walter Cronkite died late in the first decade of this millennium. From all of us in the media, in this age of emerging media, social media, and the blogosphere: good night. And go fuck yourself."

FEAR. UNBRIDLED

25

Baby Nicky is cooing, reaching for my bracelet.

"Aw…lookitthat…Tina, Doc Igno…little bro wants the bracelet…"

My favorite bracelet. Worthless to others. Priceless to me.

Each ding and scratch on this old bracelet has a story behind it. It's been in both oceans, each time late at night. Think: one of these nights you were fully clothed, the other you were completely naked except for one sock.

It gets comments from guys and girls alike for its coolness. I hand over my bracelet to Fear, who gives it to Baby Nicky. Baby Nicky gums it. I'm never touching that bracelet again.

Baby Nicky's eyes. Doped-up old people waiting their turn to die have cloudy red eyes like those, not toddlers.

I.D.K. isn't over yet. And guess what? A black dude is running for President.

Baaaack the truck up. If this black dude gets elected President—his finger is on the button—

The black dude's plight in America? I saw *Interracially-Crazed Nymphomaniac Cheerleaders Nos. 14, 16, 29, 34* and *46*—

They have all the great sports jobs, what else do they want to take from me?—

And what's wrong with e-mailing around an African tribal video with an allusion to this being that guy's Cabinet? HEY. IT. WAS. A. JOKE…—

The Internet anonymously and hatefully goes from zero to thousands—

Fear and the entire Gestapo hurtle across The Universes, returning to Earth. Fear has a ringside seat to reality. The second Fear lands on Earth, Fear wants to engage in Deduction. Deduction is kind of like the game Twenty Questions, examining stereotypes and judgments to arrive at the answer. Fear subsists on stereotypes and judgments.

Fear pledges to submerge itself in Fear's lair while sending the team out into the field. Diving into humanity, summer 2008.

Fear looks at me...

Fear instills fear through the use of dotdotdots better than any middle manager could ever wish to.

As Fear runs around Fear's lair at thousands of miles an hour to get the endorphins ready to extrapolate, the walls and ceiling and floor expand outward in each direction, digging toward the core of the Earth.

Fear's lair needs to be spherical. Seamlessness. Room to run. Must bleed off this energy. So much energy—the anonymous hate on the Internet alone is its own power line directly into Fear—feeding into Fear, must run. Fear's lair, miles below Earth, is now precisely one mile in diameter, down to the nanometer. All stainless steel. Shiny, yet stifling stainless steel. Too much energy flowing in, Fear needs to run. Fear needs emergency release valves.

Fear's desk is situated at Absolute Six, that's the six o'clock point, down to the nanometer, on the floor of the lair. The thermostat is set at two degrees below what many consider comfortable.

Fear has a high-backed leather chair. On the other side of the desk are two old low-back chairs for visitors. One has a broken wheel, which I sit in at a slight angle. The other's back keeps giving out. Sit in it too long, your lower back will be sore for a few days.

They've...they've been meaning to get those fixed...just haven't gotten around to it yet...Our sincerest apologies...Now have a seat...

Fear goes from zero to five thousand in under sixty-four milliseconds. Get the endorphins going. Bleed off energy. Think.

All angles. Ceiling, walls, floor. Fear's running track. Ceiling, walls, floor. At these speeds, slight angle changes added up to substantial directional changes very quickly.

Fear's favorite day-time reality talk show is called Humanity. Analyze humanity, its reaction, the current state of the world, and stereotype and judge and arrive at the name of the Democratic candidate for the Presidency. Fear hasn't Deducted in a while.

Fear flies at me thousands of miles an hour, stops two inches from my face.

"It's so obvious, why didn't I think of it instantly? The first President of Americanaland, only it's a black President," Fear clears its throat, for effect.

"George JaMarquiyus Washington."

No.

"Ohhhh-kay. George Larvell Washington."

No. Forget—

After another couple hundred thousand laps, Fear stops.

"George RondellDemetrius Washing—"

Forget this line of—

This chair. Lower back is going to be sore. Back pain, on top of all the fear. If Fear seems different lately, out of character, this is the twilight of the decade. It's—

"What am I doing wrong?"

All I want to do is figure out a way to get through this. Maybe Fear isn't looking at this the right way, I suggest. Maybe Fear should take a step back.

Fear boldly, pronouncedly takes a bold step back. Fear looks around.

Maybe Fear needs to take the thirty-thousand-foot view of the prob—

Subzero wind, solid sound of wind, wind and sunlight my eyes squinting—

Saying to myself: nice work, fuckhead, you and Fear are now hovering at thirty thousand feet—

Fear is looking around at the sky. And those times hearing a loud jet engine, that blip up in the sky—

A 747 thunders by fifty feet to our right at over 500 m.p.h.—

Positive spin: jet blast and vibrations destroying your eardrums also forcing you to forget that 210 m.p.h. subzero wind and lack of air freezing and suffocating—

Could have chosen your corporate-speak so much more wisely. Could—

Fear turns. The wind and jet blast go silent.

"George Thelonius Washington, Jr."

No.

"Really...Fo sho'?—"

This fleeting second—I cut Fear off. "Thirty thousand foot view" is just marketing-speak.

Whaaat? Marketing people are full of shit. We are now free-falling, back to the lair. Good, Fear isn't really feeling this whole thirty-thousand-foot thing. Brainstorming up here sucks. Fear needs to run, back in the lair.

Freefalling upside down, absorbing every second and sensation of this freefall through the sky, crashing through the ground headfirst, absorbing everything: impact and rocks and concrete and tree branches, and once again sitting in one of the uncomfortable chairs as Fear is again hurtling around the lair.

"George—"

Holy shit. Even consumed with fear, I gotta say it. I take a second to regain my composure and professionalism, then say with all due respect and sorry to not sound like a team player here, but Fear needs to try harder.

Fear stares. But Fear understands. My gamble with death worked. Fear will try harder. Fear does a couple thousand laps as I try to calm down while also figuring out how to die.

When the endorphins flow, Fear goes from brainstorm to brainhurricane.

Fear screeches to a halt two inches from my face.

"I got it—NO—I get it. His dad, who is now in jail for life, was an Asian martial arts movie freak. So he named him TaeKwanDo. This is beautiful, thisisbeautiful. I see it—As a youth, when TaeKwanDo Jackson ran with the gangs—before his spiritual awakening, that wooonnnnnnderfully life-changing jailhouse epiphany that started him on this glorious path, him putting down his AK-47 for good."

Fear starts to tear up.

"Him, getting his Bachelors Degree in prison. Making such good grades that he's offered a full ride to Harvard Law School after he's paroled. (sniff) And here it is, years later, TaeKwanDo Jackson is declaring his candidacy for The Presidency. God bless the Americanacans."

Fear is now crying. TaeKwanDo's story just stirs Fear's heart so.

No.

Though this candidate *did* get his Law Degree from Harvard. Was the first black person to chair The Harvard Law Review.

Fear looks at me…

Fear instills fear through the use of dotdotdots better than any middle manager could ever wish to.

Fear needs a margarita. Fear orders an abandoned granite quarry pit of margaritas, launches a mile into the air, lets gravity take over, lands in the middle of the quarry lake face first, and sucks down every last gallon of the margarita by the time Fear lands at the bottom, three hundred feet down.

A nanosecond later Fear is back in the lair. Fear bangs Fear's chest and lets out a belch that reverberates off the stainless steel and blows out my eardrums from every angle.

Fear needs a flowing white beard. Yes. Creatures with flowing white beards tend to know things.

Fear is thinking dis is Da Leader of Da Free World And Shit. He went to Harvard. Did good at Harvard. Fuck, Americana, this is challenging.

Fear demands to know more…

I yell out that this candidate for the Presidency had a black father, but a *white* mother.

Fear goes from thousands to zero and whispers, "Say what?"

The white beard falls out. Fear demands to know more…

His father didn't hang around long.

Fear's jaw drops to the core of the Earth. Fear demands to know more…

The father wasn't American.

Fear grows four extra sets of eyeballs to act as emergency release valves for all of this eye-popping energy.

Fear gets back to running. Fear is not brainstorming. Fear is brainhurricaning.

Endorphins must flow. Energy must be released. If asked Fear about the color barrier, Fear would reply with, "wanna fly through the center of the sun at light plus two-five?"

Those bottom-of-the-barrel reality TV shows we laugh at. That's what we are to Fear. Go into your confessional booth, shut the door and flip on the camera. Fear is watching. If Fear could comprehend diversity, Fear would give two fucks about diversity. But what Fear can't get enough of is the obsession and passion we pour into this thing called race. We are so gifted at standing still.

The 2008 Presidential Election is Fear's new obsession.

The Command Center set up in the other rooms, walls of TVs, scanning monitors, large computer screens. Teams of analysts staff Fear's War Room 24/7.

Doctor Igno and Monsieur E deploy their legions in the field.

Little Miss Doubt followed Doctor Igno's Op Team in field, though here and there she sneaks away for some good ol' fashioned Monsieur E. (They are constantly sneaking around behind Fear's back, thinking they're sly. Fear knows, but just doesn't care. We're talking about Americanaland's President here.)

She brings along many outfits, each is cut to make flashing in public as easy as possible. One is a red suit business skirt outfit with glasses to match the Republican Vice Presidential candidate. Another is a sexy Y2K-Infected Barbarian Sex Cannibal outfit.

On every street corner in America, UncertainTina is pushing Baby Nicky down the street in a baby stroller. In the stroller, with Baby Nicky, are monitoring and listening instruments, scanners, HD viewing screens—

Sensors in overdrive.

The Less sisters are deep cover. One could be the attaché to a dignitary, the other a new tour guide at The White House, the third a media mogul's new naked maid. Fear has no idea where they are, but the intel they upload via Secure Feed Victoria—Sierra Foxtrot Victor—is invaluable.

Fear likes me...feeding Fear information...For this, it's okay to full-on face-punch Sivvie. I admit: it felt good to face-punch someone. Not going crazy or anything. Just one solid face-punch once in a while.

Sivvie minds. But fuck him. He's just Sivvie. Go ahead and face-punch him right now. Why not? Throw another punch. What the hell? The economy is collapsing, trillions are evaporating, layoffs escalating. Minds that could be curing disease are devising and improvising weapons.

Punch Sivvie again. Who cares? It's just Sivvie.

Our men and women are dying in Iraq and Afghanistan. So many out of work. Industries collapsing. Debt mounting. Foreclosing. Twenty-year-old war veterans with PTSD can't get medical care. Their toddlers are on food stamps.

And a black dude—like the ones who take all the high-paying sports jobs so you can't have one—is running for President.

That guy needs to know that Old Man OlderThanDirt and that dingleberry MILF are going to kick his ass. Kick. His. Assss. I would sign this post with my real name but that black guy's army might find me so I'll sign it "KKK4Life" even though I don't *really* believe in the KKK—

The Internet anonymously and hatefully goes from—Fear goes from zero to five thousand in under sixty-four milliseconds—No way that many white people would—

Fear is now shiny bald and clean-shaven except for a pencil-thin mustache. A diamond-, ruby-, emerald-, and sapphire-studded recreation of the Presidential Seal, spherical and three inches in diameter, dangles from a gold chain molded to look like noose rope around Fear's neck. In the left ear is a diamond Air Force One earring. The two front teeth each have a gold crown, each has a single "4" set in enamel.

Fear's silk tracksuit is comprised of American flags, only the white stripes on each flag have been updated.

It's now the Red, Black, and Blue.

Fear chomps on an ear of grilled corn. I worked through lunch. The burnt husk is pulled back as a makeshift handle. A few kernels are entirely burnt. If you were being marched into a gas chamber, I say to myself, you would want this piece of grilled corn, brushed with some melted garlic butter and sprinkled with fresh-ground black pepper, to be part of your final meal. Along with the best steak you ever had.

Fear holds the corn to my face. "Bite?"

I vomit up a meal from a four-star restaurant I dined at three years ago.

Fear devours the corn, then the husk and the cob and does a few thousand more laps before stopping suddenly.

"You know what? I give up."

Fear hates to give up. Yet Fear gives up quickly and regularly. This feeling is nothing new.

I tell Fear the name of the man who is seeking The Democratic Nomination for The President of The United States of America.

Fear stops. Fear looks around the room. Are you sure that's his middle name? Fear looks down at Fear's feet, shakes Fear's head for a second. Fear starts to—that's giggling, right? Pretty much flying blind here.

Fear whispers the name, using Fear's right hand to mimic an airplane, flying through the air.

Fear is not brainstorming. Fear is brainhurricaning.

26

Fear has me triple-check that this black dude was still the President.

Then Fear wants to quadruple-check that more soldiers have indeed been killed since last time I quadruple-checked this fact.

Then Fear wants to quintuple-check the levels of fear, doubt, uncertainty, misery, and panic in the financial markets and the business world. Fear, Misery Index levels. And since I was at it, Fear also wanted me to check the latest figures on ruthlessness, relentlessness, and remorselessness. Each instrument is still reading off the charts.

Then Fear wants to sextuple-check that Einstein's Definition of Insanity is being proved and reproved and voted into law over and over again.

Fear flies around at full speed. Two inches from my face, Fear brakes and pulls its goggles up to its forehead.

"Kudos. What a worker you are. Fist pound, my friend, fist pound. And if you thought the first decade of the third millennium has been—"

In milliseconds, Fear has me cradled perfectly, tucked underneath one of its arms as we are already on our eleventh lap. The trail we leave resembles a path of electrons around an atom. Only instead of electrons, it's just Fear and I leaving this trail. And I'm not doing a thing—

—except screaming at the top of my lungs and begging for my life.

"Fist pound, my friend, fist pound."

Fear picked up fist pounding during the months leading up to the election. If the candidate-now-President and his wife can engage in this fearsome act, then by all means so can Fear.

Curvature of the room, faster, now faster—Fear says that this election, economy, these wars, gay-faggot-butt-vagina-on-vagina marriage, powerful dark-skinned people, powerful light-skinned people, dying superpowers—

Fear has to bleed off all of this energy or Fear would probably explode.

UncertainTina tells Fear they're having the best sex they've ever had.

"Fist pound, my friend, fist pound. Sorry gotta talk business on the fly."

While I am screaming, Fear says that Fear enjoys gardening. It centers Fear.

My top twenty-five most hated songs are playing right now at the same time. Each of the fifty speakers is inches from my ears.

Lap 294. Fear is most at home gazing at Fear's garden around sunset. Fear states that a cheap way to fight bugs, especially slugs, is to put little tins of subpremium light beer right by your plants. The slugs crawl in, get ripped and die.

Lap 337. SLUG BUG! Fear punches my right shoulder. Every bone in my body disintegrates then reintegrates.

Lap 373. Unbridled Fear. Fear is thinking of consulting with a planetary dynamics expert on plant and flower placement. Which calls for a fist-pound—

Lap 428. Fear says I'm hard to converse with right now. No offense.

Lap 558. Fear is ordering Chinese. Kung Pao chicken? Fear loves this place's spicy, but if you want the medium or the mild, that's cool. Low MSG though. Fear is getting a cup of wonton soup. Want one?

Lap 646. SLUG BUG! Fear punches my left shoulder. Every bone in my body disintegrates then reintegrates.

Lap 993. The Chinese delivery service orbits close to us. Fear wants to keep hauling ass, but I scream gotta lay off a bit for the delivery guy—

"YESSSS. This all makes sense now. Some random Asian dude didn't just randomly show up in the lair. Nooo. How often does that happen, unless maybe you're other Asian people or fetishists? Fear loves

Chinese, and this place's wonton soup is the best around. Yesss—smart on-the-fly thinking on this Chinese Food Issue...Plus, most delivery restaurants shit small countries when they arrive and Fear is hurtling around the lair at thousands of miles per hour. You show management potential..."

Fear throttles back, the delivery guy orbits side-by-side. Fear checks through the sack, yup, they got it all.

Lap 1529. Shitting pants for the 92nd time that day. But Fear is right: their wonton soup is fantastic.

The soundtrack of the twenty-five shittiest songs replays itself.

Lap 2042. Fear is most at home among the plants, glass of wine in hand, arm around UncertainTina, who is enjoying her glass of wine and bag of ether, the whole gang complimenting the garden. Baby Nicky, cooing and carving out lines of cocaine.

Lap 2435. I envy every soul who ever died in childbirth.

Lap 2909. Fear is tearing up. UncertainTina is more than Fear's better half. More than Fear's rock.

Lap 3218. UncertainTina, Fear sobs, is Fear's dynamic, loving, nurturing shriveled-up cum dumpster.

Lap 3391. A roller coaster times ten thousand. In the roll-around-the-track-back-seat.

Lap 4856. Fear sobs for the 1,204th time. Fear is one lucky being, with that dynamic, loving, nurturing—

Lap 4913. Fear's wish is that I find my own shriveled-up cum dumpster one day. "Fist pound, my friend, (sniff) fist pound."

Lap 5793. Fear wants to start a gardening tips website. Fear's love of gardening. A side of the Fear you thought you knew so well.

Fear likes being unbridled around you, Fear screams. Also: Fear wants to learn more about xeriscaping. And please come back after the herb garden blooms.

Full stop.

"www.takethefearoutofgardening.com. A place to share tips, bring in other gardeners, say a landscape specialist—"

Over my hysterical, sobbing protests, Fear gets moving again.

"—and the URL, being that my name is Fear. Thisisgoodthisisgood. Gotta catch the tail end of the kitsch trend before it evaporates. Gen X kitschy. The Hipsters should dig it, too."

Fear accelerates.

Lap 7764. Fear loves getting the blood flowing like this. Don't you love getting the pants-shitting going like this?

Everything I once swore I'd never say to Fear, now serenading Fear with all of—Fear cranks my twenty-five most hated songs—

We fist pound the most excruciating fist pound that's ever been fist pounded.

I don't deserve to be alive. Dante's top circle, that's where I belong. Be thankful to be in the least-miserable section of Hell.

Fear turns, makes sure I'm paying attention. Fear almost wants to stop haulin' ass. But not quite.

So Fear gets it off of Fear's chest, at lap 11,114.

"That top ring of Hell you're so wishing you were in right now at this moment, guess what? It's still Hell. Pisser."

Lap 11,694. "Doc Igno is a fantastic chef and knows a lot about wine—this is going to piss off Monsieur E, bringing Doc in, but fuck him. This is a killer last-minute, on-the-fly brainstorm—"

Why are my ears still functioning? Dumb fucking ears.

Lap 13,306. Fear is running low on barfbags. Think happy thoughts. Deep breaths.

Lap 13,802. "Watching you puke your guts out—designer barf-bags!—we start a designer barfbag company!" You and Fear! Business partners. "Designerbarfbagsmuthafucka! How many designer barfbag companies are there in the marketplace?"

Fear wants a handshake. No. Fuck that. This moment demands a fist pound. This designer barfbag venture is gonna HAPPEN.

At this point in time, I realize that Fear pretty much has no idea what a fist pound is. Fear just randomly fist pounds.

"And hey, that tiny slut little sis o' mine, she enjoys baking. Maybe a few recipes up on—Oh hey, little bro—"

Fear stops.

Every neuron absorbs this thousands-to-zero stop. The headache only begins to make itself known.

Baby Nicky waddles in, seated in his baby harness, pushing forward with bootie-covered feet. Around the rim of the tray, mounted on stakes, are doll heads.

"—you're getting SO big, baby man! It was dicey at first. Uncertain Tina and I were worried—though gotta say, The Missus and The Less Sisters wore THE sexiest white leather nurse outfits for his surgery. Black fishnet stockings—"

Fear wants to run again.

Baby Nicky murders my name in baby talk.

If soaked in gasoline right now, I would so light myself on fire.

Fear goes from zero to 68,000 in milliseconds. Those twenty-five most hated songs are back, rockin' out in unison. This is being cradled in Fear.

"And the Less sisters—"

Lap 15,682. We're on the ceiling. We're on the wall. We're on the floor.

"—But lookit that little bro of mine…"

I look. We're on the ceiling. If things were different, this would be so much fun. We're on the wall. On the floor. On the—

"Did you know that leafy plants like lettuce and spinach require more nitrogen in the soil? Fist pound, my friend, fist pound."

27

STOP DROP AND ROLL—

Y2K Fire-Breathing Flying Brontosauruses.

Y2K-Infected Barbarian Sex Cannibals Y2K Innards Falling Out Syndrome—

The Fear Index Misery Index Fire-Breathing Indexes of Misery and Fear.

Everything is stamped with The Misery Index. People's faces branded with Misery Indexes.

Over there—dotdotdots yelling LOOKATMEIFUCKSHIT.

Unpaid Overtimers all yell that, then they get laid off. Now Unpaid Overtimers are yelling it on the street.

Y2K-Infected Barbarian Sex Cannibals. The Shit-Fucking Dance.

Information Age my ass. This is The I Don't Know Decade. Is it still IDK? Is IDK over? I don't know.

Baby Nicky is there. A toddler in a neon green track suit. Dead non-toddler eyes.

All the managers and layers of managers, male, female—it doesn't matter. Interchanging each nanosecond. Baby Nicky feeds every one of them cocaine. Every worker in America forms a Shit-Fucking Dance conga-chorus line. Then the managers catch a case of Y2K Innards Falling Out Syndrome or Y2K Limbs Exploding Disease or Y2K Masturbating To Pictures of Yourself Disord—

The dance steps are one-TWO-three-four. Then one-two-THREE-four. Then all the layoffs, now it's one-seventeen-THIRTY-four. Then it's one-five-EIGHT-makeupawholenewnumber.

LOOKATMEIFUCKSHIT—wait. Layoffs.

THANKGODIHAVEAJOBINTHISECONOMY.

Three-MAKEUPANEWNUMBER-seventeen-seven.

Wait. Y2K-Infected Barbarian Sex Cannibals, Unpaid Overtimers—Y2K-Infected Barbarian Sex Cannibal Unpaid Overtimers—the connection they're combining and mutating must tell the world. Eating each other to stay employed. Mainlining Internet porn to escape. Self-destructively self-medicating. That dance, the Shit-Fucking Dance.

Every headline in the media contains the word "fear."

Y2K-Infected Barbarian Sex Cannibal Unpaid Overtimers. The Fear Index is winning. The Fear Index and Misery Index—and maybe there IS an Uncertainty and Doubt and Panic—A Ruthlessness Index—

LOOKATMEIFUCKSHIT—LOOKFUCKIATMESHIT—now they're mutating, making up new numbers, then new numbers.

New virus: Y2K Losing Belief In Optimism Disease.

LOOKATMEIFUCKSHIT, THANKGODIHAVEAJOB. Look: they have the same amount of syllables, same rhyme and cadence. The Fear Index.

LOOKATMEIFUCKSHIT, THANKGODIHAVEAJOB. There must be a connection here. LOOKATMEIFUCKSHIT, THANKGODIHAVEAJOB.

Now it's ONE-five-MAKEUPAWHOLENEWNUMBER-K—yes, the letter K. The Shit-Fucking Dance's dance steps have mutated to the point where they now contain letters.

MANAGERS SCREAMING TO LEARN HOW TO MAKE THE LETTER K INTO A DANCE STEP AND DO IT NOW TWO TRILLION DOLLARS IS SITTING OFF SHORE WHAT DO YOU HAVE TO SAY FOR YOURSELF—

Oh yeah, and the black guy is still President. Not shitting you here. He is.

Layoffs. The Fear Index—

The Fear Index, maybe they're behind the Y2K-Infected Barbarian Sex Cannibal Unpaid Overtimer mutation—and they're conspiring with the Misery Index to manipulate our markets.

Date-with-destiny morning. Rising out of the bed that hasn't been slept in for the past seven hours.

Fear's lair. How amazing it would be if neutral ground existed. Fear goes from zero to—last night, Fear killed every hero from every favorite story.

Making the appointment a few weeks back, for once Sivvie had a chance to bust chops. And boy did Sivvie bust. And what will this be about…Sivvie asks. Fear always needs to know…It's always best to have an agenda…Remembering blurting out something like THIS IS ABOUT THE FEAR INDEX YOU FUCKING ASSHOLE THIS IS ABOUT FEAR'S AGENDA NOT MINE—

Crap. Always did get low marks on Professionalism.

I download the Facepunch Sivvie App and hit "Facepunch Sivvie" repeatedly.

Sivvie cracks up even though the facepunches strike him repeatedly. Impulse control… If Sivvie were here right now I'd physically facepunch him app-punching only goes so far. What was said? Where did that memory go?

It would be so valuable to remember the exact words. And they were sure to have recorded every second.

Canceling is still an option. Sivvie had to have told Fear everything. Probably be incinerated.

Less than six weeks after the election, those who elected The President were even more fearful because their lives weren't perfect, they were consumed with Fear. And those who didn't elect him started to brag about how Fear was now their ally. They believed in Fear that much. Their faith in fear seemed to multiply each day.

Now months later, it's only—

If I don't descend into the lair of Fear for this confrontation, someone else will have to.

But aren't there more qualified people out there? Superheroes maybe?

Uncovering Fear's plans for world domination, discovering those truths behind The Fear Index, I could be killed. The Fear Index, turning us all into Y2K-Infected Barbarian Sex Cannibal Unpaid Overtimers—December 31st, 1999 was just a hoax—

These could be the final moments on Earth.

Showered thoroughly. If this is the last time showering, it is going to count.

Picked the favorite underwear. If today is the day to die, it'll be in good-looking underwear. White shirt. Red tie. Blue suit.

Sivvie just called to confirm the appointment. Of course, still can cancel...

Heading out, walking down the street, gazing up at the sun. Hey there, you ninety-three-million-mile-away-piece-of-hot-shit, if you could help here in any way—

Knowing what awaits, sooo not wanting to die yet, no chance of Heaven, want so many more decades but—

Blocks later, reaching the neverending clear glass skyscraper, ducking off the street when no one is looking and opening the keypad at the secret side door, entering the passcode.

L-O-O-K-A-T-M-E-I-F-U-C-K-S-H-I-T.

Sivvie buzzes in. Time to full-on face-punch Sivvie. Swinging as if this is the last face-punch that will ever be thrown.

Standing there, inside, waiting to descend into the lair of Fear. Punch was good. Warmup.

Sivvie descends into the lair.

After a few minutes, Sivvie ascends from the lair, holding a cloth to his cheek. Fear will see you now, Sivvie says as he spits out two of his teeth.

No pressure. Just descend into the lair of Fear, miles below the Earth.

"Fear will see you now."

You will now see Fear.

Time to descend. Fear's level of cruelty. Why?

Why do you need us to be addicted to you?

Why so much importance in misery? Panic? Ignorance? Doubt? Uncertainty? Ruthlessness, relentlessness, remorselessness?

Why is fear so worshipped? Does The Fear Index want to turn fear into a virtue?

Clank. Freshly polished shoes meet the floor of Fear's stainless steel lair.

Fear is standing behind Fear's desk, there's a peculiar smile on Fear's face. Walking toward Fear, these hundreds of yards, Fear's eyes are locked on me approaching. Fear's expression seems to say why are we having this meeting?

To the right of Fear's desk, slightly to the rear, is something new.

Sitting, staring, is a 120- to 130-pound Rottweiler/Black Labrador mix. Its eyes are locked on me as well.

Those are definitely Rott jaws. Square, ferocious jaws. The dog gets up once, does a slow circle, sits down again. It's got the Lab, bred-to-run-ten-hours-a-day body. This animal would have no trouble tracking a being down before unleashing those jaws on them.

It's jet black except for the piercing brown eyes and white diamond on its chest. Its eyes pierce.

Doctor Igno most likely has a body language specialist watching every movement over closed-circuit video. Time to speak. The dog's eyes narrow.

Fear's smile and narrowing eyes, it looks like we need to have a chat...

The Black Lab/Rott mix laser-focuses on every move.

If they find your body in a dumpster with chunks of flesh ripped away by dog teeth, full of saber or gunshot wounds and third-degree burns, at least you'll be wearing good-looking underwear.

Take a deep breath. The dog stares even more intently. Fear smiles.

Which lets out the secret: not every gambler is a winner.

"Unfasten your seatbelts: it's out past Pluto slow roll back light plus two-five straight into the center of the sun."

28

It's almost sinking in while shooting straight up through that first layer of clouds, the second, then that paper-thin third, leaving Earth's atmosphere, the full moon ahead—look back.

Unfasten your seatbelts: it's out past Pluto, slow roll back, light plus two-five into the center of the sun.

Bye clouds. Atmosphere. Curvature of the Earth. Earth. Bye forever.

Always said it made the most sense to be cremated. No need to take up a plot of land. Just didn't know that cremation would be now, and somewhere besides Earth.

Fear wants to shoot out past Pluto, then let the Sun's gravitational pull grab us for a slow roll back into the solar system before throttling up to 2.5 times the speed of light and plunging directly into the center of the sun.

Only it's not 2.5 times the speed of light. Out here, it's light plus two-five.

Nearing the Moon, the head begins to wrap itself around out past Pluto, slow roll back, light plus two-five into the center of the sun.

Sound like fun?

Unfasten your seatbelts. Incineration in million-plus-degree heat.

"Fist pound, my friend, fist pound."

Passing the Moon—it's a full Moon. Mars is ahead, small. Watching it grow, the reds separate from the pinks in its atmosphere. Red clouds.

My top fifty most hated songs are playing at the same time. Each of the hundred speakers is inches away. Fear says if we do this right, rounding Pluto is like a high jumper clearing the bar, by nanometers. A giant U-turn. Then, when the sun's pull grabs hold…

Fear says that one WAY cool thing out here in space is that everything is free.

Fear hands over the Hope Diamond. Someone call the museum guys. We're hurtling through space with the Hope Diamond. Fear says, go ahead.

"Take it. Sell it. Make some muh-fuckin money."

Hurtling forward. Time to scream. Fear isn't listening. Fear never listens—

In Fear's opinion—sorry to interrupt—humans, their fascination with visiting Mars—

"Bitch please."

Fear's middle finger is pointing toward Mars as we hurtle past it.

FYI: Fear needs to make a piss-stop on Jupiter. Gotta leak, now's the time. Nope. The sopping-wet pants and soiled-yet-good-looking underpants are just fine.

Too bad so locked up, otherwise would have noticed Jupiter's four faint rings on the approach. The star travelers call them the Jovian rings. Not nearly as pronounced as The Rings of Uranus or even a flicker compared to The Rings of Saturn, but they're there.

Would have also seen the volcano ranges—not mountain ranges, but *volcano* ranges, erupting and shooting lava hundreds of miles into space—on the surface of Io.

Io is a moon of Jupiter.

Io is larger than Earth.

Io is the most geologically active rock in our podunk solar system.

Io is beautiful this time of year.

Landing on Jupiter. Back in a sec, Fear says look around. Jupiter is beautiful this time of year. No way you're going to look around.

Fear is back. "Sorry, also took a last-minute dump."

Blasting off Jupiter, leaving its atmosphere, accelerating past Europa. Saturn and its rings are in the distance.

Faster.

Nearing Saturn, Fear farts in my face. Fear farts 4.5 on the Richter scale.

I vomit up 1987 and the last few months of 1994.

Fear noticed me shutting my eyes when I could be checking out the rings of Saturn close up. That's what prompted Fear to fart in my face. In the Universe where Fear was raised, Fear was socialized that if you want to get another being's attention, you fart in their face.

"When we round back here from the opposite direction, we should be hauling at light plus one-five."

Saturn is beautiful this time of year. Like you and your way-too-shut-eyes would know.

"I have another idea: we chloroform Sivvie, then tattoo his back with random patches of back hair. Baby Nicky will sooo be in on this."

This is what giving up hope feels—

Jolt. Big jolt.

The second Fear cut power, the Sun, 2.8 billion miles behind us, immediately exerts its gravitational pull. The best brake around.

"See you on the flip side, Uranus. That planet is beautiful this time of year, by the way. So is Neptune."

As we're slowing, Fear says, "Know what every human needs? A barcode. So, like when they're cowering in front of me, I can scan it and—of course, Fear would rather be doing drugs and having orgies with sets of triplets."

Beginning to drift around the far side of Pluto in a slow roll, right shoulder slightly higher than the left. Done right, all is dead silent. One giant U-turn: accelerate, decelerate, U-turn, accelerate.

Zero need for any thrust or countermeasure or counterthrust, cradled in the Sun's pull. Its unfathomable energy creating your flight path and bringing you around the far side in this U shape.

All you're doing is slowly rolling to your right. It's so simple. You'd be a fool to overthink this.

X axis, Y axis, yaws, pitches, just figuring themselves out.

Trajectories unfold.

Nearing the apex of the curve around the back side, halfway there. Slowing. No choreography, the slow roll, it just occurs. A host of stars serve as spectators.

Some stars live and breathe, you know.

Leaning forward, remembering going up to the top of that arch monument with Grandma, then down the other side. First, no—second grade?

Over the right shoulder, check out tiny Pluto. We who reside in this solar system should be proud. A surface of frozen nitrogen covering a layer of ice, which surrounds a core of nickel, iron and rock, Pluto makes a grand impression.

Slowing, slowing.

"Beings who can barely launch out of their own atmosphere, judging planets like Pluto, planets they could never visit. You know why? Because they're afraid, Sidney."

Pluto is like a dutiful scrappy West Highland Terrier, way out here. On guard. With a constantly wagging tail. Forever on watch, yet always ready to make a new friend.

Pluto is beautiful this time of year.

Rounding the far side of Pluto, the planet is between us and the Sun, blocking all light from the Sun. Looking over the left shoulder and darkness then—

LightpurpleDarkpurpleRedPinkBlueSkyblueFlickeringblue Flickeringorange Orang—is-that-green-maybe-could-be-know-what-let's-just-make-things-easy-and-call-it-green, yello—

spiral-shaped galaxies, nebula, cosmic bursts, starbursts—

If I had a camera along, I could snap some photos, put the space agencies and their no-talent space telescopes out of business.

Consider yourselves lucky, no-talent space telescopes.

"Twenty knots and slowing."

This slow roll is perfect. Every rotation hits at the optimum time.

The distant Sun that will pull us into itself is now a growing sunrise on the horizon of the dark side of Pluto. Fear says that the Sun—out here—it reminds Fear of a Dahlberg Daisy. Dahlbergs require less water than other types of daisies.

"This is a tightrope. A tightrope we're about to full-on sprint, in a not-actually-physically-sprinting way but this will be a tightrope-sprint nonetheless. Throttle. Surf. Afterburn."

Yet right now, at this rotational rate, Fear's and my port sides could inch alongside an imaginary dock, say ten yards ahead, toss the mooring line, then step onto the dock in one fluid motion. Out here, rounding the other side of Pluto, it sinks in.

How adrift I am.

I say to myself, you're not happy. But you got comfortable, even though this feeling doesn't resemble comfort. What does comfort mean anymore, after that decade we all went through? Why is it so similar to miserably, uncertainly, doubtfully, ignorantly, panic-strickenly living in fear?

You used to believe in yourself.

Canceling life plans, working last minute until midnight, calling this "comfortable." Comfortable. And they shut off the office ventilation and air conditioning systems at five thirty.

For most of that decade, they made you work late, and they didn't even pony up for the utility bill. And you thanked them for it.

Then you became what you became. The cruelest part about all of this is that these are now the final moments. The pull of the sun kicks in. Time to full-on sprint a tightrope into the sun.

"Know what else is kicking in?", Fear says. "That Lake Michigan of grain alcohol that I grain-alcohol-bonged back on Earth. Yup—no wait—which is a bigger cubic measurement, a Lake Erie or a Lake Michigan?"

"LAKE MICHIGAN," I scream as no one has ever screamed Lake Michigan before.

"Okay then, the Lake Michigan of grain alcohol that I grain-alcohol-bonged is kicking in. It is damned hard to find a funnel that can accommodate a Lake Michigan. Oh yeah, that Mount Evans of black tar heroin that I spiked a vein with, that's kicking in, too. And the volume of those fifty most hated songs is now at 18—no—37."

After a while, Fear needs to interrupt my screams.

"SHHH. This is important, Sidney—drunk driving—shhh, SSHH, quietshhhquietquiet—drunk driving is in-EX-Muther-Fucking-Scusa-scusable. Grainalcoholdrunk and smacked-to-the-gills space-flying at millions of miles per hours—who wegonna hit waythefuck outherehurtling throughspace?"

Fear has a confession to make. "All human dudes, human chicks, those smaller versions? What are they called again? Kids?—they all just look alike to Fear—"

Wait, Fear said this already?

"Oh. But what I didn't say before is that when those human things are cowering in front of Fear, sometimes I whiz on their backs and heads."

Instead of concentrating, Fear is demonstrating urinating on the back of humanity.

"Wee-wee-wee-wee-w—"

The Sun's pull is more than taking over.

All you can absorb about Neptune is that it is big and it is blue. Which is more than you absorbed when you were hurtling past it before, eyes mentally-stapled closed. Out here—

"A Chrysler Building of assorted painkillers would be fantastic right now, don't you think?"

Fear pops the roof of the Chrysler Building, inhales its painkiller contents, and belches at a decibel level that destroys far-off planets. I shit out my pelvic bone.

Hurtling toward the Sun.

"Last company party, Sivvie passed out. Me, Doctor Igno and Baby Nicky each got pictures of our scrote-sacks resting on Sivvie's forehead. Little Miss Doubt took the photos. Wait. Weren't you there? Didn't you get a photo?"

Those fifty songs. A hundred speakers. Fear needs to focus. Instead, Fear turns.

"Know what would be a cool side-band name? Sweat and The Glands. And Gofuck and The Yourselves, that's a cool name also."

Howling at the top of my lungs. Hurtling through space. Both Neptune and Uranus are quite large. Didn't notice on the first pass because that state of hysteria wouldn't allow it.

Fear needs to focus on plotting the jet points—

"Quit howling. Fear needs to concentrate—wait—Fuck fucking YESSSS—Sweat and The Glands should play a lightning-fast remix of 'Ninety-nine Bottles of Grain Alcohol on The Wall'—*Ninety-nine bottles of grain alcohol on the wall,*" Fear screams at the top of his lungs while snapping its fingers and bopping when Fear should be jet-pointing.

"*Ninety-nine bottles of ether and grain alcohoooool*—the distance from Uranus to Saturn is maybe 20 percent longer, but we'll still shoot the gap faster because we are HAULING ASS," Fear says.

Fear needs to focus. Fear lets the suggested calculations bounce back and—Fear has misfired before, celestial explosions and implosions weren't taken into consideration.

Concentration is critical right now.

"Take one down/Pass it around/Shoot one of those aliens with eight heads and thirty-three mouths through the face but it's cool because they grow faces back really fast/937 quadrillion bottles of blotter acid on the wall."

Fear throttles, quick short bursts.

"You know what Earth needs, Sidney? Imagine if a dog figured out how to throw its own tennis ball or stick. Wouldn't that be the LIFE? Fist pound, Sidney, fist pound."

I grab ahold of Fear and howl.

"Light plus one-two."

The speed of light, plus 20 percent.

Fear is seeing octuple right now. Saturn and its rings are growing.

"Light plus one-four."

The Sun, pulling, no bringing us into itself. Saturn and its rings, growing. Howling. Flecks of dust the size of North America give Saturn's thinner rings shape, these give the larger rings their shape.

Leaving Saturn behind—

Looking forward. Jupiter and the sun growing larger and larger. Hauling ass, throttling, surf—

"YOOOOO—right there—the Conamara Chaos Plain on the moon Europa—Sweat and The Glands and Gofuck and The Yourselves—fuck that—also The Gigantic Neo-Conical Titties, GOPublic Restroom Sex, Anus and The Titans of Methane—we're talking they play a show, a show on the Conamara Chaos plain of Europa—"

Fear knows the perfect three-thousand foot-tall ice-covered ridge, turn it into a stage.

"Quit freaking out. Wouldn't that rawk?"

Hurtling forward, looking back at shrinking Europa. That sun keeps getting bigger. Brighter. Warmer.

"Light plus one-seven."

Bye-bye, Jovian Jupiter Rings.

"This Conamara Chaos rock-out-with-your-cock-out show—It. Is. Going. To. RAWWKKKK."

Mars. Earth in the distance.

"The Lightspeed Festival!"

YESSSSSSS.

Fear bets they're going to name it The Lightspeed Festival.

Earth. Venus and Mercury. That rapidly closing distance.

"Want another hit—SHIT! ShitShitShitShitSHIT—"

Fear was thinking so much about how The Lightspeed Festival is going to RAWWWKKKKK that Fear forgot to afterburn.

Fear afterburns. Light plus one-nine. The Sun is bigger. Then bigger. Mars, twenty-three times faster than last pass other direction.

Eardrums all that sound.

Good-bye, Mars.

Speed. Heat.

Hello, Moon.

One small step for man one giant—bye, Moon.

Hello, Earth—light plus two-one—bye, Earth.

Hello, Venus. Bye, Venus.

HiMercurybyeMer—

29

Fear so fucked up.

Fear® so wants to kill Fear.

MARK THE WORDS OF THE FEAR® STAKEHOLDERSHIP: if Fear's focus-grouped, repackaged, and repositioned spiritual essence wasn't the driving force behind the Fear® brand and go-to-market strategy—if the Fear® Spring Lineup weren't about to roll out—know what?

Fear would be fucking dead.

(And don't get those thousands of departments and branch offices full of Fear® Unpaid Overtimers started. A tack hammer death beating would be fucking Heaven compared to what they would do to Fear, given the chance. Kids' birthdays, weekend plans cancelled. Though the average employee couldn't tell you who is worse: Fear, or the layers of Fear® management.)

"And you and Fear taking Fear® from 85 percent to 100 percent to 115 percent to 5000 percent to—"

As I'm coming to, the Fear® Human Resources Director stops pacing and sits down across from me in the high-backed chair, back in the lair. For me, it's back to sitting in the chair with the broken wheel.

The HR Director regains his professionalism and says thanks for allowing him to vent. The black dog is still there by the desk.

It drops the tennis ball that was in its mouth so it can pant easier.

"Sorry about that rant. I just had to cancel plans last-minute to handle this. Though I should be used to it by now. Canceled plans *are* a part of the entertainment industry. And don't worry about those guttural, coughing sounds and the retching. That's Fear getting its five stomachs pumped in the other room," the HR Director says. "Happens all the time, we just keep it quiet...Now let's see, are you a layoff or a payoff? Obviously you're a payoff. No way you could be a full-time Fear® employee. We should start screening subcontractors like we do applicants. It'll be a few minutes before the check gets cut upstairs in the Fear® Finance Department. They weren't expecting this."

At the front of the desk facing me is a manila envelope, it says "Terms of Separation." The HR Director's smartphone is next to it.

My first thought is that men as diminutive as he shouldn't wear shiny double-breasted suits.

The HR Director looks at me, clears his throat, then opens the file and starts to look at it.

"It says here you had worked with Fear® off and on in the past. But then again pretty much every person on Earth has worked for one of the countless companies underneath the Fear® umbrella at some point in their lives."

The HR Director looks up at me.

"For the record, Fear® wants it stated that everything you experienced, due to the Fear® Spokesbeing named Fear deviating from Brand Character and accidentally grabbing you instead of Sidney for a jaunt around the solar system, was indeed a departure from the Fear® Brand Promise as stated in Fear® communications efforts. In terms of your health, you were 100 percent safe cradled in unbridled Fear. In your case, hurtling out to the edge of the solar system, looping around the far side of Pluto, rocketing back by the planets, afterburning up to 2.5 times the speed of light, shooting through the center of the sun, rocketing out the other side, killing speed and break turning into Earth's orbit for a slow glide back—everything was perfectly safe the entire time.

That's one trait of being engulfed in both that being named Fear and the brand Fear®: with both of them, you're never in any danger, yet you never feel an iota of safety.

Fear® prefers it when you feel this way. Fear killed too many brain cells and can't help making you feel this way.

As a contractor, your added overexposure to 'sensitive' Fear® inside information and the B2B efforts...your previous experience...this leaves the Fear® stakeholdership in a compromising position...

Looking here at your file, when you first started subcontracting, some were so impressed with your passion and insights—especially with what you unknowingly referred to as 'fear' back then—that you were being looked at as a potential hire. It's why you were introduced to Fear itself, even though it was playing the role of Fear®, the CEO and Spokesman. Fear stayed in character then, I'm assuming."

The HR Director pauses and sends a quick text to see the status of my check, then returns to the conversation.

"Now, you're getting a nice settlement to keep quiet about the difference between Fear, Fear® and fear. From now until you die and go to Heaven, just stay silent about them. Just to clarify, and this will help you keep track in the outside world when you encounter them: the first, Fear, is a naturally shy ancient being that has lost its way. The second, Fear®, is an inferior mass-produced product that is used to control others and contributes to the first losing its way. The third, fear, exists in a tiny form within every being in the Universe and is completely natural and valuable—in small doses, that is.

The three: Fear, Fear® and fear.

After that decade, people are talking about that climate of fear or being in fear for their job. In actuality they are talking about a climate of Fear® and being in Fear® for their job. Many managers these days don't rely on fear. And God knows many don't use insight anymore. The ones I'm talking about use Fear®.

Though the inspiration for Fear® and getting people to live in Fear® was a perfectly natural spark. In fact, that mirror feeling within, which you called fear, is a positive force, in small amounts.

And Fear itself was at one time just a mild-mannered being. Out there in the Universe, Fear's job title used to be Reality Check Compliance Officer."

The dog woofs, wags her tail, whimpers. The HR Director shooshes her.

"In a bit, Sidney. Little Miss Doubt or Baby Nicky will take you on an s-p-a-c-e-r-i-d-e in a bit. Riled up dogs undermine the atmosphere of professionalism Fear® strives for, this will never be one of those dog-friendly company cultures. This, I'm assuming, is Fear's passive-aggressive intent. Get under Fear® management's skin. Yes, the political, passive-aggressive gestures around Fear® are as childish as any corporation. Back to Fear: before Fear® began, as our Reality Check Compliance Officer, Fear was a being all of us met with only on occasion. Fear was never meant to run everything, especially not be the CEO of our lives.

Fear possessed a talent, a spark. For millennia, this spark helped beings across the universe step back and see different troublesome entities or situations for what they truly were. Your RCCO didn't force one decision or another, just merely lit up the different possibilities with that delicate spark called fear. And unlike Fear®, Fear always treated you with respect and intelligence.

But that spark Fear possessed, that spark was identified as something to be leveraged. Could Fear's spark be used to appeal to the lowest common denominator, the worst in beings? Is there a collective fear that's rooted in the worst of all of us? All of these were asked.

Was there a collective fear? If so, could this collective fear be tapped into and manipulated? Fear, only pumped with preservatives, derivatives, additives—"

The HR Director grabs the vibrating smartphone, looks at the e-mail screen, hits a few keys, then puts the phone down.

"Back to this. This will help you out there, since you'll now see the Fear® brand for what it is. This spark, Fear's essence, was mass-produced, commoditized. Into Fear®. Fear® was packaged in multiple ways—liquid forms, pill forms, wearable forms that created feelings of self-consciousness, spun off into different types of services, flooding the airwaves and media. A B2B Initiative was created to look at tapping into the Leadership Development Market and that effort skyrocketed. Fear® was diversified and sub-targeted to different groups in ways to further fit their lifestyle within the larger go-to-market strategy to appeal to the collective worst in all of us.

Fear® went to market. A lowly, quiet being named Fear was bought off, then thrust into the limelight. Its essence monetized and staring down at you from billboards until you looked away. The floodgate-opener for Fear® was the B2B realm discovering its potential for leadership and companies ordering palettes upon palettes of it.

After the launch, Fear was thanked, paid well, then politely asked to disappear. Fear® was everywhere, body doubles were in place at every branch office and media station, and they no longer needed Fear.

Fear would have stayed four Universes away, too, engaging in alien sex orgies and drug marathons. But something happened.

An American citizen born in the State of Hawaii named Barack Hussein Obama ran for President. Fear heard that this candidate's chances of winning were strong."

The dog woofs again. After shushing Sidney, the HR Director continues.

"Fear, knowing humans the way Fear did, thought about this. The first eight years of that decade, Y2K before that—and now THIS? Fear hurtled back through many galaxies and returned to Earth. When it landed, Fear was barraged with Fear®.

Since Fear had been away, Fear® messaging and promises had been manipulated, amplified, mutated, and experimented with even more by its stakeholders—maximum Fear® profitization.

All of those messages about the power of Fear®, the pervasiveness of Fear®, newspaper headlines talking about Fear® controlling the world, Fear® in self-help articles, giant flashing billboards of Fear®, Fear® all over the airwaves—Fear bought that Fear® Go-To-Market Strategy hook, line, and sinker. More than all of us combined. Fear couldn't remember penning any of those words or painting those pictures or posing for those flattering photographs, but every one of them made so much sense.

Fear waltzed into the Headquarters of Fear®, thanking everyone and signing unasked-for autographs and announcing that the all-seeing, all-powerful Fear® was back in control. All the Fear® body doubles were relieved. The real Fear® was back.

Fear stormed into the Fear® Leadership Seminars and took the presentations over from the bewildered Fear® speakers and suggested to female attendees that they stand and stretch and that's not alcohol they smell is Fear® getting too close hey let's do some jumping jacks!

A consultant, way out of its league as CEO, only with no idea and there was no way anyone could explain any of it to Fear at this point. See, the Fear® enterprise was also such a house of cards that attempts at stifling all of this could easily call attention to the many inconsistencies of Fear®. Though contingency funds aside, Fear® is still substantial."

The HR Director pauses and looks at the file on the desk. "Which you will be well compensated to keep quiet about... —sorry, the dotdotdots just slip out sometimes.

Another thing: look at the average corporation. With their 'fiefdoms' and 'cutthroat politics' and 'eat-you-alive corporate culture,' they aren't that different from Fear®. Actually, companies and people that use those terms seriously are tremendous consumers of Fear®. Fear® must be protected at all costs. If anything, from Fear.

For example, you probably don't remember what happened when it was announced that Fear® was the Number One Brand in the Universe. No one remembers it.

Operation Humanity Mind Erase was a success.

Finance is slow, I'll see what's up with that check then tell you all about the Operation. Why not? After seeing the dark side of Pluto, knowing about this can't hurt. Actually, it's good, this will reduce the amount of surprises for you once you're in the outside world. Fear®lessness is a different feeling, I'm told."

The HR Director leaves, but leaves his smartphone on the desk.

After two minutes of hearing Fear retch and go on about how The Lightspeed Festival is going to RAWK, the HR Director's phone vibrates and the e-mail in-box light appears. Even with Sidney staring, I still reach across the desk and pick it up.

The e-mail is from the Fear® Legal Department.

The subject line is: NEW FEAR®/FEAR DISCLOSURE POLICY...

Figures. In this business climate nowadays, it's all about covering your ass. Keep the information surrounding an operation like this tight. And with the web, this could get out. Smart move on the part of the Fear® lawyers, tightening their disclosure policies.

I hit 'erase.'

30

The HR Director returns, with an overnight envelope tucked underneath his arm.

"Your check isn't ready. No new messages. Where were we? Operation Humanity Mind Erase. That was after it was announced that Fear® had become the Number One Brand in The Universe. Thanks to Operation Humanity Mind Erase, the Fear® Unpaid Overtimer legions of spin doctors, P.R. folks, marketers, mind manipulators, administrators, waterboarders, and lawyers saved the day for the Fear® stakeholders. This is good, this will prepare you because Fear will probably pull something again.

After the Number One announcement, Fear® crafted a speech, loaded with dotdotdots, to capture the essence of this moment. Fear was instructed to memorize it.

It went something like, 'Not to detract from my competitors...my competitors...though I am sure they're going to supplant my number one position by this time next year (chuckle, chuckle)...I am humbled... I am...I am...truly honored...'

But Fear—still trying to wrap its head around how it single-handedly worked its magic to become the Number One Brand in spite of those unnecessary suits getting in Fear and Fear®'s way—thundered through the aisles of Fear®'s press conference thinking 'No WAY Fear® wastes time memorizing some speech. That battalion of prostitutes is waiting, Fear®, let's do this. Fear® soaks in the magic of this moment, grabs the microphone and—'

Fear stomped onto the arena stage, soaked in the magic, grabbed the microphone, and screamed, 'Suck my genital-wart-covered, syphilitic dick then die in an acid-fire while getting gang-assraped in a heap of herpes-infected-corn-filled diarrhea-shit all you shitfucking pants-shitty second-, third-, and tenth- place hack-job no-talent giraffe-molesting homo-fuckers who thought you had a right to be the number one brand, FuckBITCHES! FEAR® OWNS YOU. FEAR®—'

The speech went on like this, for the next five thousand and two minutes.

And it only got more vulgar.

Every human, every consumer of Fear®, saw it. Fear and Fear® were on every station, Website, every event on Earth cut away to this Fear® press conference.

For three hours alone, Fear went on about what Fear® was going to do to Glenn Beck for hacking its mojo.

Fear® tried to pull the plug, but all of you saw it. Do you know why no one remembers anything?

Because of the power of Fear®.

At that moment when the Fear® team of commandos stormed the press conference and shot Fear with over five billion tranquilizer darts, everyone was horrified. Only no one remembers because the Fear® Damage Control Department more than earned their pay—even though they didn't technically earn one penny of overtime. A regular occurrence at Fear® is canceling your weekend plans and putting your life on hold. Yes, just like any company nowadays."

Sidney barks and the HR Director shushes her.

"And of course, there was also Operation Memory Forget, Operation Counteract Image of Fear's Scrotum—countless others. You, though, your condition is irreversible, being no longer able to live in Fear®. You're not fearless, just Fear®less. What you could tell the world, this makes you a concern for Fear®…"

The HR Director stops for a second and shakes his head. "What am I doing using dotdotdots with you? You OD'ed on Fear®, now it's powerless.

And you'll probably also see Fear, Doctor Igno, the whole gang, out and about in multiple forms, acting very unlike the brands of Fear®, Ignorance®, Uncertainty®, Panic®, Misery®, Doubt®, Ruthlessness®,

Relentlessness®, and Remorselessness® that you have come to know in this new millennium. All you have to do is remember the money you were paid and not say a thing to those who still see them through the appropriate lenses.

As I was walking back here, I remembered something. While you were catatonic, you babbled on about The Fear Index. Make your life easy: The Fear Index is a monetized mathematical derivative traded on the stock market that bases its worth on implied volatility. There is no conspiracy named The Fear Index. And we don't like to think of Fear® as a conspiracy...rather...an opportunity to be leveraged...Brought the dotdotdots back for a second to drive the point home.

Though an interesting similarity exists: The Fear Index *trades* on implied volatility, the Fear® brand *capitalizes* on implied volatility. But Fear, in believing all of its manufactured Fear® hype, is now creating levels of *actual* volatility the original Fear® stakeholders never imagined."

The HR Director gives an I-only-work-here shrug.

"But still, all of the chaos that comes with operating such a complex behemoth, the first decade of the new millennium was still very good to Fear®. How good? Fear® just slashed its marketing budget to zero.

Because of The I Don't Know Decade, Fear® is the very first self-sustaining brand. As for your silence—"

From the back room, Fear coughs and begins another round of dry heaves that vibrate the stainless steel. Sidney barks one quick bark.

The Director chuckles, "It's okay, Sidney, someone will take you for that s-p-a-c-e-r-i-d-e that Fear screwed up. Good girl." The HR Director shakes his head. "There was a perfectly obvious reason that Sidney was staring at you before: you might be a cat. Sidney thinks everything is potentially a cat. A tree could be a cat. A rock or asteroid could be a cat. A quasar could be a cat. Throughout The Universe, Sidney must forever remain vigilant when it comes to the cats. When you and Fear shot off into space, her thought was that maybe you went out to tell all the other cats that now is the time."

Sidney woofs her confusion, which the Director answers with a shush.

"The only reason she ventured over here to see Fear was that her favorite beings, like Optimista, her sidekick Joyy, the mischief-loving Miss Chiv, Elatia, Old Man Happs, even Spire and his inspiring aura—none of them were around. Just Fear and the emotional beings you know already. I don't think Optimista and her crowd seem to be making themselves known. And none of them are the type to ever sell their wondrous sparks for the sake of profits. Not like Fear. What a funny entity. Fear is the head of this mega-corporation, yet hates the artificial lighting of an office more than any being, derisively calls it 'UO Light,' for Unpaid Overtimer. Between you and me, Fear tried calling in sick again today. This just started happening."

Sidney picks up the ball and continues to stare.

"That dog isn't even Fear's. It's just one of the quintillions of beings wandering out there throughout the Universes. I'm assuming you'll see more. It's part of the 'no longer able to live in Fear®' thing which I'll never experience."

The Director chuckles again. "And for your sake, good thing you weren't awake when you and Fear landed back on Earth. Fear, oblivious to the chaos it just caused, landed on the landing platform, then looked at the crowd of angry Fear® Unpaid Overtimers who just cancelled their plans to deal with this. Fear turned to ask Sidney if she—and Fear saw you instead. Then Fear remembered that Fear® had some meeting today.

Fear thought about you, unknowingly hurtling through space, due to Fear's unthinking insensitivity. It was the first time Fear ever saw a human as something more than an amusing plaything."

The dog cocks its head. The HR Director continues.

"Then Fear thought about it more. And grabbing you on accident was 'the shit-all, balls-to-the-wall, silliest, funniest thing' Fear had ever heard in Fear's millennia of existence. You, out there, hurtling forward at millions of miles an hour, seeing those planets up close—only with zero clue any of it was about to happen. Then going catatonic—Fear's hysterics sounded like every ounce of laughter from every commentator or Website that targets and ridicules a particular disadvantaged group— homeless people, the disabled, people from third-world countries. And all of that was directed at you. Then Fear thought, what if you didn't force yourself to go catatonic? What if you were awake while hurtling through the center of the Sun, watching the laws of physics mutate and self-reinvent and disintegrate—Fear's laughter mutated and amplified."

The Director stifles his inadvertent chuckling.

"As annoyed as I was at canceling my own plans, I did see the humor in it. Fear paraded your catatonic body around the landing platform yelling, 'Look at me! I'm Mr. Spaceman! Look at me! I'm Mr. Spaceman!' Fear farted in your face. As Fear started to go on about some Lightspeed Festival, the substances kicked in. Fear stumbled and started projectile-vomiting, the Fear® Paramedical Team was airlifted in."

The HR Director looks at me, chuckles, shakes his head for a second, then picks up the envelope on the desk and looks at it.

"Oh, this was lightspeeded over while you and Fear were about four-fifths of the way through the Sun. We frown on contractors using our address. Your company name though…sounds familiar—"

The HR Director's phone rings. He picks it up and on the other end is Doctor Igno, UncertainTina, Monsieur E, all screaming. Baby Nicky is wailing. The HR Director starts to tremble, then says, "Yesyes, I'll be right there" as he gets up and begins to straighten his suit before turning around to run out. His eyes were getting wider and wider the whole time he was on the phone.

Gotta watch that disclosure, homie. These days, corporations are all about covering their asses. Despite what their commercials say, even Fear® isn't above those forces.

I reach over to pick up the envelope, but do this slowly.

Sidney is still there.

Remember, I might be a cat.

31

Dear CEO, Egan® Disciplinary Fish Food,

We just saw the product launch video that you shot this weekend and posted on the Internet this morning.

At the beginning, when that chorus line of fish in the aquarium started spasming and screaming "Look at me! No prob-lem!", we were confused. Then, we saw it. We really and truly saw it.

A brand centered on giving people who live in fear a little experience of being on the other side of fear. Leveraging the power of fear, genius.

We had this offer lightspeeded over because we're buying Egan®. R&D. Distribution and Merchandising Rights. Graphics. Brand Equities. Your idea of a fleet of planes with "Egan® light-up banner thingies trailing behind them," we're looking into it. We're bringing Doc and Egan® on board, too. That gigantic plastic bird's knowledge of Generally Accepted Accounting Principles and SEC Compliance is astounding.

Enclosed is a check for thirty-one million dollars.

In Egan®, we see a business opportunity that will help us hang on to the six hundred workers we were going to let go. Disciplinary fish food could be a transitional business for us. Expand into other segments of Fish Food, maybe even give up the Disciplinary market altogether. Maybe its core equities won't be as valuable one day... (These aren't "Hey look! We're being dicks!" dotdotdots, we're just thinking.)

And if you know of any ventures in the Neon Rock or the Miniature Ceramic Pirate Ship Industries, we're looking to invest in those business arenas as well.

We're taking Egan® from here. You're no day-to-day CEO. We'll call you for DFF Strategization and Brainhurricanization Consultations, but otherwise stay away. Our security force is armed.

Good work, Job Creator. Sincerely,

Harland Lamar Beauregard Tobacco, Inc.

P.S. We just made a company Intranet posting with our new corporate vision: "It's time to revolutionize!!! Forget cigarettes, addict them to pets!"

32

Thirty-one million dollars.

Egan, wherever you are in the Heavens know this my friend: your kids are going to college.

I look at that check again. That third kid, she better start cracking the books now. She's got the dough to study Accounting, Literature, Law, *and* Lightspeed Breaking.

In the other room, Fear's retching now mixes with the HR Director's screams for mercy.

If it weren't for Sidney and all of that commotion, it would be time to do a dance in the name of college funds. Make up the steps as I go. And unlike The Shit-Fucking Dance, this dance would make sense. Even if the steps didn't, the dance itself would.

But I sit still. According to Sidney, I might be a cat.

That Separation Agreement, the Fear® check. I just want to forget those and bolt out of here with the thirty-one million dollars to deposit in my checking account. But then again, the Fear® money—

The level of anguish in the HR Manager's sobs grows.

This level of anguish mixes with Fear's guttural stomach-pumping sounds. Footsteps pounding—not out of the woods—wait a minute—

Wait a—

Doctor Igno, Little Miss Doubt, UncertainTina carrying Baby Nicky, Monsieur E, and The Less Sisters thunder in at, crowd around the desk, hovering and circling it. Doctor Igno reaches and grabs the Separation Agreement off the desk.

Doctor Igno, Little Miss Doubt, and UncertainTina's eyes narrow. Baby Nicky smiles. The Less Sisters collectively stare. Monsieur E reaches inside his black leather trench coat.

Maybe consider giving the Egan® money, as a bribe—but no—

Been out past Pluto and back, through the center of the Sun catatonic, realized that the company where you toiled as an Unpaid Overtimer earlier in the decade didn't even respect you enough to pay the utility bill and you were far too thankful for this and mistook this for comfort, shat and pissed self a couple of hund—

From beneath the trenchcoat, Monsieur E pulls out a manila check envelope and hands it over. UncertainTina, who for once isn't schnockered on crystal meth, says on one condition... must absolutely solemnly and utterly swear...

"We added to your settlement based on the extra unintended disclosures. But you must never utter another word about Fear®. Or it's spokesbeing, the once mild-mannered Reality Check Compliance Officer and shitstick of a husband named Fear. Or living in Fear®. Or the difference between fear and Fear®. Many entities are heavily invested. And you especially cannot say anything about Optimista, Joyy, Miss Chiv, Spire, Old Man Happs, or Elatia. Or the fact that there are trillions upon quintillions of other beings and creatures out there, wandering and meandering and hurtling throughout The Universe, beings who have a thing or two in common with Earthlings. Or anything else pertaining to this whole subject. You must raise your hand and solemnly swear to Fear®. This is non-negotiable. Not. One. Word. Ever."

These beings don't seem to be familiar with the whole signing-things legal protocols we have on this planet. More proof that Fear® and the forces behind it aren't what they advertise themselves to be. Must tell the world.

Even better, they don't know about the Egan® dough.

Set up those kids' college funds, send some to Egan's wife, way nice chunk left over to set up some more college funds for some more unwanted kids, then later on set up some more college funds for other unwanted kids—plus Fear® wouldn't own me.

From the other room, Fear's guttural sounds meld with the HR Manager's sobs and they echo off the stainless steel. Like Fear®'s former HR Manager, it would be best for me to be out of here. Walk away now, but still—

Decisions. Decisions—is their money really—then again it's obvious that check—

Or be free to tell the whole world about the difference between fear, Fear and Fear®—

Decision time. I had to do it. I couldn't help opening the envelope and looking at the enhanced severance.

So many more zeroes. Enough to complicate things—

Who are you kidding? Take their money. Anyone would.

Wait. That idea sucks. Here's a better one: take their money AND the Egan® money AND be free to tell the whole world about the difference between fear, Fear, and Fear®.

I've honored Fear® and its contractual obligations enough. Even after those many times when Fear® failed to live up to its end of the bargain.

If Doc were here, he would tell me to wield my powers of Legaleselessness.

I looked at each of them, crossed my fingers behind my back, then solemnly swore that I would never, ever say another word about Fear®. Ever.

I even shook each one's hand to show how serious I was. They applauded. Throughout I Don't Know, it's been a pleasure doing business, I said. My fingers were still crossed.

Two minutes before they catch on, tops. Time to saunter back toward that hundreds-of-yards-away door. Ascend from the lair with both of these envelopes, straight to the bank PRONTO—

Wait, now they're talking about cocktail hour? Turning that down would invite suspicion...

How to sneak out of here. That door, those hundreds of yards between me and that door.

Oh yeah, one more thing: the bank is about to close. Forgot.

No way anyone would hold on to two checks for this many millions over the weekend. Countries could rob this money. Need a smokescreen—I may have some powers of Legaleselessness, but I don't have the power to stop the bank from closing. No one has that power—

Need a distraction. Anything. Both Doctor Igno and UncertainTina look over. Need—

The perfect distraction drops her tennis ball and wags her tail.

"HEY SIDNEY WANNA HAUL ASS AT LIGHT PLUS TWO-FIVE STRAIGHT THROUGH THE CENTER OF THE SUN THEN GO CHASE A GAGGLE OF CATS?"

Half a nanosecond after I yelled then 180ed and high-tailed it towards that exit, Sidney shot forward from her sitting position. As she subconsciously charged forward, all 120 pounds of her lost their footing on the stainless steel and slid into Doctor Igno.

More accurately, she slid into the right knee he had replaced not too long ago.

As Doctor Igno was on the ground writhing, Sidney attempted to get up and gotupfelldowngotupfelldown three times before catching her feet again. Then it occurred to Sidney that besides being Ride Day, this is also Tennis Ball Day.

Sidney loves it when Ride Day and Tennis Ball Day are The Same Day.

Sidney's howls and frantic clawing on the stainless steel barraged Baby Nicky's sensitive ears, he yelled and screamed hysterically. Monsieur E and Little Miss Doubt and The Less Sisters leapt at Sidney and missed, landing on the stainless steel with a thud, their foreheads knocking into each other. UncertainTina screamed and ranted at the pile of all of them.

The employees of Fear® prairie-dogged from their cubicles for a moment.

Sidney then danced the Sidney-Is-Going-To-The-Sun Dance and howled the It's Ride Day And Tennis Ball Day Song.

Back to me:

Sprinting those hundreds of yards, now reaching the door, ascending from the lair of Fear®.

Shit. The bank is closing. Fear® could put a stop to that check at any second. And who knows with the Egan® money. Ascending. Won't sleep until this money clears.

Ascending upward from the lair of Fear, just get these checks in the bank today.

Won't sleep until this money clears. Hurry. Might turn myself in—or not—right after setting up the college funds and some do-good-type of fund with the Fear® money, but not thinking about that now.

Ground floor.

Sivvie looks up from the lobby desk, then tenses up. Though I have no desire to face-punch, just race past him to the bank.

Reaching the outside door. Shit, the bank is about to close. Just reach it before—

Wait.

The Egans, the Fear®'s, and the ellipses-slinging middle managers of the world didn't force. They gave me a choice.

I'm the one who chose to punch Sivvie.

I had the Egan® money. Plus, my fingers were crossed behind my back.

So I took out the Fear® hush money and signed it over to the worker who deserved it. Sivvie. The Egans of the world would never do that. Then again, they're going to Heaven and I'm not. They can achieve true fearlessness. All I have is Fear®lessness.

Did you hear the HR Director's comment about seeing through Fear® until that day I die and go to Heaven? I don't fault him. He didn't know—

The bank. Next thing I did was scream at Sivvie to get his ass to the bank and Fear® could put a stop on that check any second and he had better tear out that door like a motherfucker right NOW—

Out the door. Down the sidewalk. SHIT.

The bank is about to close. How does one deposit a check for thirty-one million dollars?

Hum-dee-dum, it's just me and my check for thirty-one million dollars for my checking account, got a pen?—sprinting down the sidewalk to the bank. Then, sprinting faster.

Endorphins flowing. As I'm sprinting, Egan® check clenched in my right hand, I'm not brainstorming.

I'm brainhurricaning.

About Optimista.

And her partner in crime, Joyy. And Miss Chiv.

They sound hot...

(BTW: just thinking here. And BTW: all three are SMOKIN' hot.)

Spire. Elatia, sounds like an elating being. And Old Man Happs, huh? Definitely happy.

I find a way to sprint even faster because I gotta make the bank. Maybe that cute teller is working. Me, barging in there, in this ripped up filthy suit, filthy yet best-looking underwear, huffing, puffing. Handing over this check for thirty one million dollars.

Imagine the look on her face.

I find a way to sprint faster because of the looks I'm getting from the Y2K-Infected Barbarian Sex Cannibal Unpaid Overtimers.

It's time to revolutionize, sprint faster.

Imagining Sidney's howls as she's shooting through the center of the Sun with the inconvenienced being taking her on this ride. Hopefully it's Baby Nicky. Them landing back on Earth, her ecstatically licking his bald zombie-toddler face as a thank you to him for this much-needed cruise around the solar system.

I sprint because there's a chance that your twenty-five or fifty most hated songs, all played at the same time, would converge and merge into the most soul-stirring sound you ever heard.

Music is based in numbers: beats, rhythm, two-four and three-four and four-four time. Beats are common across all songs. How far-fetched is the idea that these songs could weave together in some unimagined way that blows your mind with a sound you've never heard before, that will never leave your head and transform the ways your brain process the very concepts of sound and harmony and beauty?

Far-fetched? Far-fetched is far different than impossible.

Gotta make the bank.

I sprint because I just figured out Old You. Old You isn't your old self, at some younger point in time. It contains the energy from that physical part of you, yes, along with what was most vibrant, only combine this vitality with all of the ancient wisdom and experience that has existed in your soul since the dawn of time. Old You is the being at that intersection.

For all of its wisdom, Old You is a fragile being. Respect it. My Old You no longer exists. Yours does.

Wind breezes across my face.

I find ways to sprint faster because I'm going to make the bank. That cute teller will be working. And I will be her next customer.

Two random lines of a poem:

And I sprint faster because Earth is beautiful this time of year/

I sprint because this beats walking on eggshells head down in fear—

It's a start. Who knows? And HELL no. I'm not going to recite these lines to that bank teller. Why recite poetry when you have a check for thirty-one million dollars?

Story title: *Sidney Saves The World From The Cats.*

Or what about this: a new brand of superhero. One that can keep up with the gone-craziness of our world—

Hurtling through the center of the Sun fried his brain but infused him with radiation that helps him eradicate bullshit and move this world forward.

Mr. Spaceman.

That might be trademarked, I'll have to consult with Doc so he can wield his all-knowing powers of Legaleselessness to figure this matter out. Or how about this—

A worldwide, underground conspiracy exists. The Fear Index.

The Fear Index is everywhere and nowhere. The stakeholders will stop at nothing to seed fear, doubt, panic, ignorance, uncertainty, and misery. Ruthlessness, relentlessness, remorselessness.

But The Fear Index has a problem.

His nanosecond flirtation with the dark side of Evil destroyed his mind and damned his soul but he is forever optimistic.

He loves Old You with all his heart because his Old You is gone forever.

He talks to ghosts, channels influxes of energy from other Universes, knows the difference between fear Fear, and Fear®—connects with intra-Universal forces like joy, mischief, inspiration, happiness, elation—

Need a name—an insanely optimistic new word created from two negative words.

Fearkiller.

Yeah.

Hang on—*Fearkiller?*

Can't we leave that brand of fear behind us?

If not, then look around.

Brainhurricane with me.

Besides fear, doubt, uncertainty, panic, misery, ignorance—check out all those other forces—

If we have Fearkiller we need Anxiety Assassin, InsecurityIncinerator, Miss Punisher of Paranoia—

Lady NervousNuker.

Time to kick negativity's ass.

Alert The GloomAndDoom-Destroying HottieTwins, Trepidation Terminator, Vindictiveness Vampiress, The Conquistador of Conflicted Feelings—

Invite others. This group isn't exclusive. Just make sure everyone is insanely optimistic and no one masturbates to pictures of themselves.

Can't think of this group as crime fighters. Calling them superheroes doesn't feel right—

They could be a band—

A band of revolutionaries?

No.

Revolutionizers.

They aren't out to overthrow anybody.

But they also know something and aren't afraid to say it:

Inside every Y2K-Infected Barbarian Sex Cannibal Unpaid Overtimer is an Old You.

Old You is fearless.

Chris Maley lives in Denver, Colorado. This is his first novel.

www.chrismaley.com
Photo: David Pahl, David Pahl Photography
Cover Art: Justin Hayes

Made in the USA
Charleston, SC
18 October 2012